—— Louisa May ——
Alcott

# LITTLE
# WOMEN

# Contents

| | |
|---|---|
| *To the Reader* | 5 |
| *About the Author* | 7 |
| *Four Sisters* | 9 |
| *A Merry Christmas* | 22 |
| *The Laurence Boy* | 38 |
| *Being Neighbourly* | 52 |
| *Beth's Piano* | 68 |
| *Thin Ice* | 80 |
| *Fine Feathers* | 98 |
| *Secrets* | 118 |
| *A Telegram* | 134 |
| *Dark Days* | 146 |
| *Laurie Makes Mischief* | 162 |
| *The Last Drop* | 172 |
| *Aunt March settles the Question* | 184 |

# To the Reader

When you have seen and enjoyed a film or TV programme that has been made from a famous book, you may decide to read the book.

Then what happens? You get the book and, it's more than likely, you get a shock as well! You turn ten or twenty pages, and nothing seems to *happen*. Where are all the lively people and exciting incidents? When, you say, will the author get down to telling the story? In the end you will probably throw the book aside and give it up. Now, why is that?

Well, perhaps the author was writing for adults and not for children. Perhaps the book was written a long time ago, when people had more time for reading and liked nothing better than a book that would keep them entertained for weeks.

We think differently today. That's why some of these wonderful books have been retold for you. If you enjoy them in this shorter form, then when you are older you will go back to the original books and enjoy all the more the stories they have to tell.

# About the Author

Louisa May Alcott was born in 1832 in Pennsylvania, the daughter of the American philosopher and poet, Bronson Alcott. She was educated mainly at home, and later served as a nurse during the American Civil War.

Like Jo, her heroine in *Little Women*, she was determined to write from a young age and, as a result of various well-meaning but expensive philanthropic and educational schemes devised by her father, she became for a time the family's bread-winner, writing her first book when she was only sixteen. *Little Women*, set at the time of the Civil War, was first published in 1869 and was an immediate success. She wrote various other popular books, including two sequels to *Little Women*, *Little Men* and *Jo's Boys*. She died in 1888.

# Chapter One
## *Four Sisters*

It wanted three days to Christmas.

The small American town where the March family had their home lay hushed and still under a blanket of snow that had lain over all the countryside for weeks past; snow that seemed as settled as the sadness in the hearts of so many American women in that winter of 1861 – the sadness of knowing that Christmas had come round once more, with their menfolk still away fighting in the terrible Civil War that raged to and fro across the hills and plains of their great land.

The four March sisters knew something about that sadness. They sat at home in the twilight before a crackling fire.

"You know, Christmas won't be Christmas without any presents," grumbled Jo, who was lying on the rug.

"It's so dreadful to be poor," sighed Meg.

Little Amy sighed and sniffed. "I don't think it's fair for some girls to have lots of pretty things, and other girls nothing at all," she said sorrowfully.

"We've got Father and Mother and each other, anyhow," said Beth from her corner.

"We haven't got Father," said Jo, "and we shan't have him for a long time."

The four young faces darkened at the words. Nobody spoke for a minute. They were all thinking of Father, far away where the fighting was.

They made a pretty picture, sitting there in the firelight. Meg, the eldest, was sixteen: a fair, plump girl with large eyes, plenty of soft brown hair and a sweet mouth. Fifteen-year-old Jo was tall and thin and brown. She had a comical nose, grey eyes, big hands and feet, a flyaway look to her clothes, and the appearance of a girl who was shooting up into a woman and didn't like it. Beth was a rosy, smooth-haired girl of thirteen, with a shy manner and a quiet voice. Amy, who had blue eyes, was pale and slender and had long yellow curling hair.

Meg sighed again and said, in an altered tone, "You know why Mother doesn't want us to have presents this year. It's going to be a hard winter for everyone, and she thinks we ought not to spend money for our own pleasure, when our men are suffering in the Army. We ought to go without *gladly* – but I'm afraid I can't!"

She shook her head, thinking sadly of all the pretty things she wanted – and wouldn't get.

"Well, we've each got a dollar," cried Jo. "I don't expect anything from Mother or you, but I *would* like to buy something for myself. I'm sure we've worked hard enough to earn it."

"I know *I* have – teaching those dreadful children all day!" said Meg.

"You don't have half such a hard time as I do," answered Jo, indignantly. "How would *you* like to be shut up for hours with a fussy old lady like Aunt March, who keeps you trotting to and fro the whole time?"

"What about me?" cried Amy. "You don't have to go to school with girls who laugh at your dresses, and label your father if he isn't rich—"

"If you mean *libel* then say so, and don't talk about *labels* as if Father's a bottle of pickles," said Jo, laughing.

"I know what I mean," Amy snapped.

"Be quiet, girls," said Meg. "Don't start fighting. Try to be ladylike."

Jo at once sat up, put her hands in her apron pockets, and began to whistle through her teeth.

"Jo, don't!" cried Meg. "It's so *boyish*!"

"I know," answered Jo, simply. "That's why I do it. I always wanted to be a boy. I'm dying to go and fight with Father – and I have to stay at home!"

The clock struck six. Mother would soon be home from her work at a club for wounded soldiers.

Beth rose, swept up the hearth, and put a pair of slippers down to warm. Meg got up and lit the lamp, Amy arranged the cushions in the easy chair, and Jo sat up to hold the slippers nearer to the blaze.

She frowned. "These slippers are quite worn out," she

said. "Mother *must* have a new pair. I'll buy her some with my dollar."

"No, I shall!" cried Amy.

"I'm the man of the family while Father is away," said Jo, "and *I'll* get the slippers."

"I'll tell you what," said Beth. "Let's each get Mother something for Christmas, and not bother about things for ourselves."

"Yes!" cried Jo. "I'll get the slippers. What will you others buy?"

Everyone thought for a minute.

"A pair of gloves," said Meg at last.

"I'll get her some handkerchiefs," said Beth.

"And I'll get her a bottle of cologne," said Amy. "She likes it, and it won't cost much, so I'll have some money left to buy something for *me*."

Jo got up and began marching up and down with her hands behind her back. "We'll surprise her," she said. "We'll have to go shopping tomorrow afternoon, Meg. We've still got a lot to do about the play for Christmas night."

"It'll be the last time I do any acting," answered Meg. "I'm getting too old for such things."

"You're the best actress we've got," said Jo warmly. "We ought to rehearse tonight. Come here, Amy, and do the fainting scene. You're as stiff as a poker when you fall!"

"I can't help it," said Amy, ruefully. "I'm not going to

make myself all black and blue, tumbling about the way you do. If I can't go down easily, then I'll have to fall into a chair."

"Do it this way," said Jo. "Stagger across the room, crying frantically: 'Roderigo! Save me! Save me!'"

She tottered across the room, hands clasped, and with a scream that was truly thrilling.

Amy tried to copy her, but poked her hands out stiffly before her and jerked herself along as if she went by machinery. Her "Ow!" had nothing of fear in it: it sounded as if someone had stuck a pin into her.

Jo gave a long groan, Meg laughed, and Beth – who was making toast – let her bread burn as she watched the fun.

"Oh well," said Jo, "you'll just have to do the best you can. Come on, Meg, let's run through your part."

The rehearsal went on until Jo, as the villain of the play, died in agony, of poison.

"That's the best we've done it yet " said Meg, as the dead villain sat up and rubbed his elbow.

"Jo, I don't know how you can act so well and write such splendid things!" exclaimed Beth.

"I do think *The Witch's Curse* is the best thing I've written yet," said Jo. "But I'd like to try *Macbeth*. I've always wanted to do the killing part." She rolled her eyes and clutched at the empty air before her. "'Is this a dagger which I see before me?'" she cried.

"No," said Meg, "it's the toasting fork with Ma's shoe on it instead of bread."

The rehearsal ended in a general burst of laughter.

"Well, I'm glad to find you so merry, girls," said a cheerful voice at the door.

They all turned to welcome their mother – a plump lady whom they thought the most splendid woman in the world.

"And how have you all managed today?" asked Mrs March. "Has anyone called, Beth? Meg, how's your cold? You look tired, Jo. Amy, come and give me a kiss."

While she was speaking she got her wet things off, her warm slippers on, and sat down in the easy chair. The girls flew about trying to make things comfortable for her. Meg set the tea table; Jo brought wood and pulled up chairs, dropping, overturning, and clattering everything she touched; Beth trotted to and fro between parlour and kitchen; while Amy gave directions to everyone as she sat on her mother's lap with folded hands.

When they were gathered around the table Mrs March said, with a happy face: "I've got a treat for you after supper."

A quick, bright smile went round like a streak of sunshine. Beth clapped her hands and Jo cried: "I know – it's a letter from Father!"

"Yes, a nice long letter. He's very well, he says, and sends all sorts of loving wishes for Christmas."

Mrs March patted her pocket as if she had treasure.

"Hurry up and get done," cried Jo, choking on her tea, and dropping her bread, butter side down, on the carpet in her haste to get at the treat.

"I think it was splendid of Father to go as a chaplain when he was too old and not strong enough for a soldier," said Meg warmly.

"When will he come home, Mother?" asked Beth with a little quiver in her voice.

"Not for many months, dear, unless he's sick. Now come and hear the letter."

They all drew near to the fire, Mother in the big chair and Beth at her feet, Meg and Amy perched on either arm of the chair, and Jo leaning on the back.

Very few letters written in those hard times were not touching in some way, especially those which fathers sent home. This one, however, was a cheerful, hopeful letter, and only at the end did the writer's heart overflow with fatherly love and longing for the little girls at home.

"Give them all my dear love and a kiss," he wrote. "Tell them I think of them by day and night. I know they will remember all I said to them, that they will be loving children to you and do their duty faithfully, so that when I come back to them I may be prouder and fonder than ever of my little women."

Everybody sniffed when they came to that part, and

even Jo wasn't ashamed of the great tear that dropped off the end of her nose.

"I'll try not to be rough and wild in future," she said. "I'll try to do my duty here, instead of always wanting to be somewhere else."

"That's a good idea," said Mrs March with a smile. "We'll see how much you've improved before Father comes home again."

"We ought to have a roll of directions, like Christian in *Pilgrim's Progress*," said Jo, thoughtfully.

Mrs March smiled again.

"And so you shall have," she said. "Look under your pillows on Christmas morning, and you will each find your guidebook."

CHAPTER TWO

## A Merry Christmas

Jo was the first to wake in the grey dawn of Christmas morning.

She sat up and looked round. No stockings hung at the fireplace, and for a moment she felt disappointed. Then she remembered her mother's promise, slipped her hand under her pillow, and drew out a little book with a crimson cover.

She opened it. It was a New Testament – that beautiful old story of the best life ever lived, and Jo knew what her mother had meant when she said that each girl should have a guidebook.

She woke Meg with a "Merry Christmas" and told her to see what was under her pillow. Another New Testament came out, this time with a green cover. They woke Beth and Amy, who found their little books also – one dove-coloured, the other blue; and all sat talking about them while the east grew rosy with the coming day.

"Where's Mother?" asked Meg, as she and Jo ran down to the kitchen to thank her for their gifts, half an hour later.

Hannah looked up from her cooking, frowning. She had lived with the family since Meg was born and they all thought of her more as a friend than a servant.

"Goodness only knows where!" she replied. "Some poor creeter came a-beggin', and your ma went straight off to see what was needed. There never *was* such a woman for givin' away food and clothes and fire wood!"

"She'll be back soon, I guess," said Meg. "You'd better do your cakes and have everything ready."

She and Jo went into the living room to look over the presents they had bought, which were in a basket hidden under the sofa.

"Where's Amy's bottle of cologne?" asked Meg, surprised. "It's gone."

"She took it out a minute ago and went off with it," replied Jo, dancing about the room to take the stiffness out of the new slippers.

"Don't my handkerchiefs look nice?" asked Beth, coming into the room. "I marked them all myself."

A door slammed and steps sounded in the hall!

"Here's Mother! Hide the basket, quick!" cried Jo.

There was a rush to hide the basket. It was only Amy, however. She came in hastily, and flushed when she saw her sisters there.

"Where have you been? And what are you hiding behind you?" asked Meg, surprised to see by her hood and cloak that lazy Amy had been out so early.

"Don't laugh at me, Jo," said Amy. "You know I only bought that little bottle of cologne? Well, I've been out to change it for a big one, and I gave *all* my money to get it – and I'm not going to be selfish any more."

She showed, as she spoke, the handsome flask that replaced the cheap one.

"Amy, you're a trump!" cried Jo.

There was another bang of the street door. This time it *must* be Mother. The girls flew to the table, eager for their breakfast.

"Merry Christmas, Mother! Thank you for our presents," they cried in chorus.

Mrs March beamed at them, still wearing her outdoor clothes. "A merry Christmas, girls," she answered. "Now,

listen, please. I want to say one word before you sit down. Not far from here lives a poor German woman named Hummel. She has a little newborn baby, and in her house there are six children huddled into one bed to stop them from freezing, for they have no fire. They've nothing to eat either, and the oldest boy came to tell me that they were suffering badly from cold and hunger. Look, girls, would you like to give them your breakfast as a Christmas present?"

There was a little silence. All the girls were very hungry, having waited nearly an hour. Then Jo exclaimed, remembering her mother's Christmas gift:

"Of course, Mother. I'm so glad you came before we began."

The others were already gathering up food to pack into a basket. Mrs March smiled happily and proudly.

"I knew you'd do it," she said. "When we come back we'll have bread and milk for breakfast, and make up for it at dinner time."

They were soon ready. With Hannah they went through back streets so that few people saw them.

A poor, bare, miserable room they found at their journey's end; with broken windows, no fire, ragged bedclothes, a sick mother and wailing baby, and a group of pale, hungry children cuddled under one old quilt.

How the big eyes stared and the blue lips smiled, as the girls and their mother entered.

"Ach, mein Gott! It is good angels come to us!" exclaimed poor Mrs Hummel, crying for joy.

Hannah made a fire and stopped up the broken window panes with old hats and her own shawl. Mrs March gave the mother hot soup, while the girls spread the table, set the children round the fire, and fed them like so many hungry birds.

It was a very happy breakfast, though the girls had none of it. When they went away there were not in all that town four merrier people than those hungry girls who had given away their breakfasts on Christmas morning.

Back home again, they set out their presents while their mother was upstairs.

"She's coming! Strike up, Beth! Open the door, Amy! Three cheers for Mother!" cried Jo, prancing about, while Meg went to lead Mother to the seat of honour.

Beth sat at the piano and played a mery march. Mother smiled and her eyes were full as she looked at her presents and read the little notes which went with them. The slippers were put on at once, a new handkerchief was slipped into her pocket – well scented with Amy's cologne – and the gloves proved to be a perfect fit.

After that, the girls spent most of their time getting ready for the evening performance of Jo's play.

Presently a bell sounded, the curtains flew apart, and the play began. The scene was "a gloomy wood". Jo, playing the part of Hugo, the villain, stalked in with a

clanking sword at her side, wearing a black beard, a long cloak and a pair of russet leather boots. Hugo sang of his hatred for a certain Roderigo, and his love for a young lady named Zara. He planned, it soon became clear, to kill the one and win the other. At last he stole to a cave and ordered Hagar, the witch, to come out.

Out came Meg, with grey horsehair hanging about her face, wearing a red and black robe, carrying a staff, and with strange signs upon her cloak. Hugo asked for a charm to make Zara adore him, and a poison to destroy Roderigo. Hagar promised both.

In reply to a chant from Hagar a little figure in cloudy white waved a wand, sang a snatch of song, dropped a little bottle at the witch's feet and vanished. Then an ugly black imp popped up with a bang, croaked a reply, tossed a dark bottle at Hugo and disappeared. Hugo went off with his bottles, while Hagar told the audience that as he had killed a few of her friends in times past, she had put a curse on him and meant to have her own back.

The curtain fell on that dramatic note. A good deal of hammering went on before the curtain rose again. A tower now rose to the ceiling; halfway up appeared a window with a lamp burning at it, and in the window stood Zara, waiting for Roderigo. He came, wearing a plumed cap, a red cloak, and the same boots that Hugo had worn. The two sang of their love for each other, then Zara agreed to run off with her lover.

Then should have come the grand effect of the play.

Roderigo produced a rope ladder with five steps to it, threw up one end and asked Zara to come down. Timidly she crept out of the window, put her hand on Roderigo's shoulder, and was about to leap gracefully down, when she forgot her train. It caught in the window; the tower tottered, leaned forward, fell with a crash, and buried the unhappy lovers in the ruins!

A shriek went up as the russet boots waved wildly from the wreck, and a golden head emerged, exclaiming: "I told you so! I told you so!"

With wonderful presence of mind Don Pedro, the cruel father of Zara, rushed in and dragged out his daughter, with a hasty aside to the audience: "Don't laugh! Act as if it was all right!"

The play went on and reached its end without further mishap.

Then Hannah appeared with "Mrs March's compliments, and would the ladies walk down to supper?"

This was a surprise even to the actors; and when they saw the supper table they looked at each other in happy amazement. There was ice cream – both pink and white – and cake, and fruit, and bonbons, and in the middle of the table four great bouquets of hothouse flowers!

It took their breath away. They stared first at the table and then at their mother, who looked as if she was enjoying herself immensely.

"It's Santa Claus," said Beth.

"No," replied Mrs March. "Old Mr Laurence sent it."

"The Laurence boy's grandfather?" exclaimed Meg. "Why, we don't even know him!"

"Hannah told one of his servants about your breakfast party. He's a strange old gentleman, but that pleased him. He sent a note this afternoon, saying he hoped I would let him show his friendly feeling towards my children by sending a few trifles in honour of Christmas Day."

"That boy put it into his head, I know he did! I wish I could get to know him," said Jo, as the plates went round and the ice cream began to melt out of sight.

"You mean the people who live in the big house next door, don't you?" asked one of the girls. "Mr Laurence keeps his grandson shut up and makes him study hard. We invited him to our party, but he didn't come. Mother says he's a nice boy, though he never speaks to us girls."

"Our cat ran away once, and he brought her back. We talked about cricket and so on over the fence, and were getting on capitally, when Meg came and he walked off. I'm sure he needs fun," said Jo decidedly.

"He brought the flowers himself," said Mrs March, "and I should have asked him in if I'd been sure what was going on upstairs. He looked so wistful as he went away, hearing the fun and not having any of it himself."

"We'll have another play some time," said Jo, "and he can see that. Maybe he'll help act; wouldn't that be jolly?"

Meg examined her flowers with interest. "I never had a bouquet before. How pretty it is," she said.

Beth pressed her face into her posy. "I wish I could send them to Father," she said softly. "I'm afraid he isn't having such a merry Christmas as we are."

## CHAPTER THREE
# The Laurence Boy

"Jo! Jo! Where are you?"

It was Meg, calling from the foot of the garret stairs.

"Here," answered a husky voice from above.

Meg ran up the stairs and found her sister, reading and eating apples, wrapped up in a comforter on an old three-legged sofa by the sunny window. It was here that Jo liked to sit with a book.

Meg waved a letter in her sister's face. "Such fun!" she cried, and then read from the paper with girlish delight:

"'Mrs Gardiner would be happy to see Miss March and Miss Josephine at a little dance on New Year's Eve.' Mother says we may go – but what shall we wear?"

"Our poplins," answered Jo, with her mouth full, "because we haven't anything else. Yours is as good as new, but I've got a burn and a tear in mine. What am I going to do about that?"

"Sit still as much as you can and keep your back out of sight," said Meg. "The front's all right."

"Then I'll stay still," said Jo. "I don't care much for dancing. Don't worry about me. Go and answer the letter and let me finish this splendid story."

Meg went away to "accept with thanks".

A large part of New Year's Eve was spent by Meg and Jo in "getting ready for the party". Meg wanted a few curls about her face, and Jo undertook to pinch the papered locks with a pair of hot tongs.

"Ought they to smell like that?" asked Beth anxiously from her perch on the bed.

"It is a queer smell!" said Amy. "Like burnt feathers."

"Don't worry," said Jo. " I'll take off the papers and you'll see a cloud of little ringlets."

She put down the tongs and took off the papers, but no cloud of ringlets appeared. The hair came with the papers, and the horrified hairdresser laid a row of little scorched bundles on the bureau before her victim.

"Oh, oh! What have you done? I'm spoilt! I can't go! My hair, oh, my hair!" wailed Meg, looking with despair at the uneven frizzle on her forehead.

"I'm sorry," groaned Jo. "The tongs were too hot, and so I've made a mess."

"It isn't spoilt," said Amy. "Just frizzle it, and tie your ribbon so that the ends come on your forehead a bit. I've seen lots of girls do it that way."

"Serves me right for trying to be fine. I wish I'd left my hair alone," cried Meg sadly.

"It'll soon grow out again," said Beth, and that was Meg's only comfort.

She was dressed and finished at last. The family between them got Jo's hair up, and her dress on. Meg was in silvery grey with a blue velvet snood, lace frills, and a pearl pin borrowed from Mother; Jo in maroon, with a stiff linen collar, and a white chrysanthemum or two for her only ornament. Meg's high-heeled slippers were too tight and hurt her, though she would not own it; and Jo's nineteen hairpins all seemed stuck straight into her head, which was not exactly comfortable.

"Have a good time, dearies," said Mrs March as the sisters went daintily down the drive. "Don't eat too much supper, and come away at eleven when I send Hannah."

The girls stood, twenty minutes later, in Mrs Gardiner's house, feeling a little timid, for they seldom went to parties. Mrs Gardiner, a stately old lady, greeted them kindly, and handed them over to the eldest of her six daughters. Meg knew Sally Gardiner, and was at her ease very soon; but Jo, who didn't care much for girlish gossip, stood with her back carefully against the wall. No one came to talk to her, so she just stared at people rather forlornly till the dancing began, and then slipped into a curtained recess, planning to peep and enjoy herself in peace.

Unfortunately, another bashful person had chosen the

ame hiding place. As the curtain fell behind her she
ound herself face to face with the "Laurence boy".

"Oh, I didn't know anyone was here," she stammered.
She was backing out again as speedily as she had
ounced in. The boy looked startled and then laughed.

"Don't mind me," he said. "Stay if you like."

"Shan't I disturb you?"

"No, I only came in here because I don't know many
people."

"So did I," said Jo, and then, trying to be polite and
easy: "You live near us, don't you?"

"Next door," he said, and laughed again.

So did Jo, heartily. She liked this boy, she decided.

"We had such a good time over your nice Christmas
present," she said.

"Grandpa sent it."

"But you put the idea into his head, didn't you, now?"

"How is your cat, Miss March?" asked the boy, his black
eyes shining with fun.

"Nicely, thank you, Mr Laurence. But I'm not Miss
March, I'm only Jo."

"And I'm not Laurence, I'm only Laurie."

"Laurie Laurence – what an odd name!"

"My first name is Theodore, but I don't like it – the
fellows called me Dora, so I made them say Laurie instead."

"How did you make the boys stop calling you Dora?"

"I thrashed 'em. Don't you like to dance, Miss Jo?"

"I like it if there's plenty of room and everyone is lively. In a place like this I'm sure to tread on people's toes, or do something dreadful. That's a splendid polka they're playing. Why don't you go and try it?"

"I will, if you'll come too," he answered, and gave her a little bow.

"I can't. I told Meg I wouldn't, because—" She stopped, wondering whether to tell.

"Because what?" asked Laurie curiously.

"You won't tell?"

"Never!"

"Well, I've a bad trick of standing before the fire, and so I burn my frocks, and I scorched this one. It shows, and Meg told me to keep still so that no one would see it. You may laugh if you want to; it *is* funny, I know."

But Laurie didn't laugh.

"Never mind that," he said. "There's a long hall just out there, where we can dance and no one will see us. Please come!"

Jo went gladly. The hall was empty and they danced a grand polka. When the music stopped they sat on the stairs and talked, until Meg appeared in search of her sister. She beckoned, and Jo reluctantly followed her into a side room, where Meg collapsed on to a sofa, holding her foot and looking pale.

"I've sprained my ankle," she said. "That stupid high

heel turned and gave me a horrid wrench. I don't know how I'm going to get home. As soon as supper is over, watch for Hannah, and tell me the minute she comes."

"I'll get you some coffee," said Jo, and went blundering away to the dining room. Someone bumped into her as she lifted a cup of coffee, so that it spilt and made the front of her dress as bad as the back.

"What a blunderbuss I am!" she exclaimed, scrubbing at the gown with her glove.

"Can I help you?" asked a friendly voice, and there was Laurie, with a full cup in one hand and a plate of ice in the other.

"I was trying to get something for Meg, who's very tired," answered Jo, glancing dismally at her stained skirt.

"I was looking for someone to give this to; may I take it to your sister?"

"Oh, thank you! I'll show you where she is. I won't offer to carry it myself, for I shall only spill it if I do."

Jo led the way. They found Meg, and Laurie drew up a little table, then fetched more coffee and an ice for Jo and stayed talking to them.

They had quite a merry time until Hannah appeared. Meg forgot her foot and rose so quickly that she was forced to catch hold of Jo, with an exclamation of pain.

"Hush! Don't say anything," she whispered, adding aloud: "It's nothing. I turned my foot a little, that's all," and limped upstairs to put her things on.

Jo decided to take matters into her own hands. She slipped outside, found a servant, and asked if he could get her a cab. A second later Laurie, who had heard what she'd said, came up and offered his grandfather's carriage, which had just come for him, he said.

That settled it. In no time Meg and Jo were rolling away in the fine closed carriage, with Laurie sitting up on the box so that Meg could keep her foot up, and the girls were able to talk over their party in freedom.

"I had a fine time. Did you?" asked Jo.

"Yes, till I hurt myself. Sallie's friend, Annie Moffat, asked me to come and spend a week with her when Sallie does. It'll be wonderful if Mother only lets me go," said Meg, cheering up at the thought.

Then Jo told Meg of her adventures, and by the time she had finished they were at home. They said "Good night", with many thanks, and crept into the quiet house.

"It really seems like being a fine young lady to come home from a party in a carriage and sit in my dressing gown with a maid to wait on me," said Meg, as Jo bound up her foot and brushed her hair.

"I don't believe fine young ladies enjoy themselves a bit more than we do in spite of our burnt hair, old gowns and tight slippers that sprain our ankles when we're silly enough to wear them," said Jo.

And, in that, I think she was quite right.

## Chapter Four
# Being Neighbourly

"Oh, dear, how hard it seems when holidays end!" sighed Meg.

"I wish it was Christmas or New Year all the time," answered Jo, yawning dismally. "Ah, well, we'll have to be like Mother and put up with it without grumbling."

They went down to breakfast. Everyone seemed rather out of sorts and inclined to croak. Beth had a headache and lay on the sofa; Amy was fretting because she'd not done her homework; Jo *would* keep whistling and made a great racket getting ready; Mrs March was very busy trying to finish a letter which had to go at once; and even Hannah had the grumps.

"There never was such a cross family!" cried Jo, losing her temper after she'd upset an inkstand, broken both boot lacings and sat down on her hat.

"And you're the crossest person in it!" returned Amy, on the verge of tears.

"*Do* be quiet, girls," cried Mrs March, crossing out the third spoilt sentence in her letter.

At last Meg and Jo and Amy were ready. They all turned at the gate and waved to their mother who, as always,

was at the window to nod and smile and wave a hand to them. They parted for the day, each going off and trying to be cheerful in spite of wintry weather and hard work. For them the New Year was really under way.

When Mr March had lost his property in trying to help an unfortunate friend, the two eldest girls had begged to be allowed to do something to help support themselves. Meg had found a place as a nursery governess. She found life harder to bear than the others because she could remember a time when it had been much easier.

Jo happened to suit Aunt March, who was lame and needed an active person to wait upon her. The old lady, who was Father's sister, wouldn't speak to the family at all for a time, after the trouble, but then had met Jo at a friend's house and taken a fancy to the girl's comical face and blunt manners. She had asked for Jo as a companion, and the girl, although her life was full of trials, rather liked the peppery old lady, and the thought that she was doing something to support herself made her happy.

Beth, who was a housewifely little creature, stayed at home and helped Hannah, while Amy, who was still at school, was never so happy as when drawing. She was in a fair way to being spoilt, for everyone petted her and her small vanities and selfishness were growing nicely.

They all, however, had one thing in common. They found it hard to settle back to work after the delights of the holiday.

Luckily, however, there was always Saturday to look forward to . . . .

One snowy Saturday afternoon Meg found Jo clumping through the hall in rubber boots, old cloak and hood, with a broom in one hand and a shovel in the other.

"What are you going to do now, Jo?" she asked.

Jo looked at her, a mischievous twinkle in her eyes. "Going out for exercise," she answered.

"It's cold out," said Meg with a shiver. "You'd do better to stay dry and warm by the fire."

"I don't like to doze by the fire," answered Jo. "I like adventures, and I'm going to find some."

Meg went back to toast her feet and read a book, and Jo went out into the garden to dig paths with great energy. Only a low hedge at the edge of the garden separated the March house from that of Mr Laurence.

Since the Gardiner's party Jo had been eager to make friends with the "Laurence boy".

While she was digging she saw old Mr Laurence drive off and then sallied out to dig her way down to the hedge. She paused when she was almost there and took a quick look round. All was quiet; the curtains were down at the lower windows; and she could see nothing but a curly black head at an upper window, looking wistfully into their garden, where Beth and Amy were snowballing.

"There he is," thought Jo. "I'll toss up a snowball and then have a word with him."

Up went a handful of soft snow, and the head turned at once, the mouth smiling. Jo nodded and laughed, and waved her broom as she called out:

"Hello! What are you doing inside? Are you sick?"

Laurie opened the window and croaked out as hoarsely as a raven: "Better, thank you. I've had a cold and been shut up a week."

"Isn't there some nice girl who'd read and amuse you?" asked Jo. "Girls are quiet and like to play nurse."

"Don't know any girls."

"You know me," began Jo, then laughed and stopped.

"So I do! Will you come, please?" cried Laurie.

"I'm not quiet and nice, but I'll come if mother will let me. I'll go and ask her. Shut that window, like a good boy, and wait till I come."

Laurie closed the window as she ran towards her house. In a little while there came a loud ring at the front door, then a decided voice asking for "Mr Laurie". A surprised-looking maidservant came running up to announce a young lady.

Jo appeared, her face all rosy, and with a covered dish in one hand. "Here I am," she said briskly. "I've brought you some of Meg's blancmange. I couldn't refuse, she was so anxious to do something for you. Tell the girl to put it away for your tea. What a cosy room this is!"

"It might be, if it was kept nice. It's supposed to be my study, but the maids are lazy and won't keep it tidy."

"I'll put it right in two minutes," said Jo, and bustled round the room, tidying, laughing and talking, and in a few minutes had whisked things into place and given quite a different air to the room.

"How good you are," said Laurie. "Please take the big chair and let me do something to amuse my visitor."

"No," answered Jo. "I came to amuse you. Shall I read?"

"No, thank you. I'd rather talk."

"Well, I'll talk all day if you'll only set me going. Beth says I never know when to stop."

"Is Beth the one who stays at home a good deal?" asked Laurie with interest.

"Yes, that's her."

"And the pretty one is Meg, and the curly-haired one is Amy, I believe."

"How did you find that out?"

Laurie coloured up a little. "Well, you see, I often hear you calling to one another when you're in the garden. I can't help looking over at your house. You always seem to be having such good times. Sometimes I can see into the window where the flowers are, and when the lamps are lighted I see you all round the table with your mother. I can't help watching. I haven't got a mother, you know."

The lonely look in his eyes went straight to Jo's heart.

"I do wish you'd come over and see us sometimes," she said. "Mother is so splendid she'd do you heaps of good. Wouldn't your grandpa let you?"

"I think he would, if your mother asked him," said Laurie, his face brightening. "Only he doesn't like me to be a bother to strangers."

"We aren't strangers, we're neighbours – and you wouldn't be a bother. You ought to go out more."

"Well, you see, Grandpa lives among his books and doesn't go out very much. Then Mr Brooke – he's my tutor – doesn't live here, so I can't go out with him."

"I'll see that Mother invites you to our house one day. Never mind being bashful – it won't last long if you keep on coming."

Laurie turned red again and quickly changed the subject. They got to talking about books, and to Jo's delight she found that Laurie loved them as well as she did and had read even more than herself.

"You must come and see our library," he said, getting to his feet. "Grandpa is out, so you needn't be afraid."

"I'm not afraid of anything," returned Jo, tossing her head.

"I don't believe you are!" exclaimed the boy.

He led the way to the library, where Jo clapped her hands and pranced, as she always did when specially delighted. It was lined with books from floor to ceiling, and there were pictures and statues, cosy easy chairs, and strange tables and bronzes; and, best of all, a great open fireplace with quaint tiles all round it.

Jo sank into the depths of a velvet chair. "Laurie," she said, "you ought to be the happiest boy in the world!"

Laurie shook his head. "A fellow can't live on books," he said.

Before he could say any more, a bell rang and Jo flew up in alarm.

"Mercy me!" she exclaimed. "It's your grandpa!"

Laurie gave her a wicked grin. "What if it is?" he asked. "You're not afraid of anything, you know."

The door opened and a maid appeared. She beckoned. "The doctor to see you, sir," she said.

"I must see him," Laurie said to Jo. "I'll have to leave you for a minute."

"Don't mind me," answered Jo. "I'll be all right."

Laurie went away and his guest amused herself looking at the books and pictures. She was standing before a fine portrait of Laurie's grandpa when the door opened again. Without turning, she said: "I'm sure now that I shouldn't be afraid of him, for he's got kind eyes, though his mouth is grim, and he looks as if he had a strong will of his own. He's not as handsome as *my* grandfather, but I do like the look of him."

"Thank you, ma'am," said a gruff voice behind her.

She swung round and there, to her great dismay, stood old Mr Laurence.

Jo's cheeks were on fire. For a minute a wild desire to run away possessed her but a second look showed her that there was a sly twinkle in the old gentleman's eyes. The gruff voice was gruffer than ever, after that dreadful

pause, when he said: "So you're not afraid of me, hey?"

"Not much, sir."

"And you don't think I'm as handsome as your grandfather?"

"Not quite, sir."

"But you like me in spite of it?"

"Yes, I do, sir."

That answer pleased the old gentleman. He gave a short laugh, shook hands with her and, putting his finger under her chin, turned up her face and looked at it gravely. He let it go and said, with a nod: "You've got your grandfather's spirit, if you haven't his face. He *was* a fine man, my dear, and I was proud to be his friend. Now, what have you been doing to this boy of mine, hey?"

"Only trying to be neighbourly, sir." And Jo told how her visit had come about.

"You think he needs cheering up a bit, do you?"

"Yes, sir."

"Tut, tut, there's the tea bell. You must stay and have it with us."

The old gentleman threw open the library door at the same moment that Laurie came running downstairs. The boy halted with surprise at seeing his grandfather.

"I didn't know you'd come, sir."

"That's clear by the way you racket downstairs. Come to tea, sir, and behave like a gentleman," said his grandfather.

He turned then to Jo and offered her his arm with old-fashioned courtesy. It was, for Jo, a wonderful moment. Before the boy's wide-eyed gaze, the two walked on arm in arm, and Jo's eyes danced with fun as she imagined herself telling the story at home.

## CHAPTER FIVE
# Beth's Piano

The tale of Jo's adventure *did*, indeed, create a sensation among her family. They all found something very attractive in the big house on the other side of the hedge. Mrs March wanted to talk of her father with the old man who had not forgotten him; Meg longed to see the fine furnishings; Amy was eager to see the pictures and statues; while Beth sighed for the grand piano.

Jo had told them about the piano, which stood in the great drawing room.

"After tea," she said, "I asked Laurie to play – and so he did, very well indeed. Yet all the time I had the feeling that his grandfather didn't like to see him at the piano – and didn't like to admit that Laurie could play so well. Now, why should he be like that, Mother?"

"I'm not sure, but I think it's because his son, Laurie's father, married an Italian lady, a musician, which dis-

pleased the old man. He never saw his son after he was married. The boy's parents died when he was only a little child, and then his grandfather took him home. I expect the old man is afraid that the boy may want to be a musician. At any rate, I expect Laurie's skill reminds him of the woman he did not like."

"How silly!" said Jo. "Why not let him be a musician if he wants to?"

And there the matter was left.

Two days later old Mr Laurence called himself to see them. He talked over old times with their mother, said something funny or kind to each of the girls, and nobody felt much afraid of him except timid Beth.

A friendship sprang up between the two families and flourished like grass in spring. What good times the girls and Laurie had! They staged plays of their own making; went for sleigh rides and skating frolics; passed pleasant evenings in the old parlour; and sometimes went to merry little parties at the great house.

Jo spent a lot of time in the library and amused the old gentleman with her criticisms; Amy copied some of the fine pictures and enjoyed beauty to her heart's content; and Meg could walk about the great house as much as she liked.

Only Beth, who loved music and was longing to try the grand piano, could not pluck up courage to go to the mansion. She went once with Jo, but the old gentleman

had stared at her so hard from under his heavy eyebrows, and said "Hey!" so loudly, that he frightened her until her "feet chattered on the floor", she told her mother. She'd never go there again, not even for the piano.

In some mysterious way, Mr Laurence learned of her fears and made up his mind to mend matters. During one of his brief calls he led the conversation to music, and talked about great singers he had seen, fine organs he had heard, and told such charming stories that Beth crept nearer, as if fascinated. She listened at the back of his chair, her eyes wide open and her cheeks red with excitement. Mr Laurence took no more notice of her than if she had been a fly. Presently, as if the idea had just come to him, he said to Mrs March:

"Laurie doesn't bother about his music, now. The piano is suffering for want of use. Wouldn't some of your girls like to run over and practise on it now and then?"

Beth took a step forward. The thought of that splendid piano quite took her breath away.

Before Mrs March could reply, Mr Laurence went on with an odd little nod and a smile: "They needn't see or speak to anyone, but run in at any time. Please tell the young ladies what I say, and if they don't care to come, why, never mind."

Here, he rose, as if going. Beth made up her mind to speak. A little hand slipped into his, and she looked up at him with a face full of gratitude.

"Oh, sir!" she said. "They do care, very, very much!"

"Are you the musical girl?" he asked gently.

"I'm Beth. I love music dearly, and I'll come if you're quite sure nobody will be disturbed."

She trembled at her own boldness as she spoke.

"Not a soul, my dear. The house is empty half the day, so come and drum away as much as you like."

"How kind you are, sir."

Beth blushed like a rose under the friendly look he wore. The old gentleman stooped down and kissed her.

"I had a little girl once with eyes like these," he said softly. "God bless you, my dear. Good day, madam," and away he went in a great hurry.

Next day Beth crept in at a side door of the Laurence house, and made her way as quietly as any mouse to the drawing room. Quite by accident, of course, some fairly easy music lay on the piano; and, with trembling fingers and frequent stops to listen and look about, Beth at last touched that wonderful instrument. At once she forgot her fear, herself, and everything else but the delight that the music gave her.

After that she slipped through the hedge nearly every day, and the great drawing room was haunted by a tuneful spirit. She never knew that Mr Laurence often opened his study door to hear the old-fashioned airs he liked; and she never suspected that the exercise books and new songs which she found in the rack were put there for her.

"Mother," she said, a week or two later, "I'm going to make Mr Laurence a pair of slippers. He's so kind to me I *must* thank him, and I don't know any other way."

All the sisters helped choose the pattern for the slippers and to buy the material. Beth started work and was at it early and late, with some help over the really hard parts.

As soon as the slippers were finished, she wrote a very short, simple note, and, with Laurie's help, got them smuggled on to the study table one morning before the old gentleman was up.

For two days nothing happened. On the afternoon of the second day Beth went out to do an errand. As she came back she saw four heads popping in and out of the parlour window; the moment they saw her several joyful voices screamed: "Here's a letter from the old gentleman; come quick and read it!"

Her sisters seized Beth at the door and led her to the parlour in a triumphant procession, all pointing, and all saying at once: "Look there! Look there!"

Beth looked. She turned pale with delight and surprise. There stood a little cabinet piano, with a letter lying on the glossy lid, directed like a signboard to "Miss Elizabeth March".

"For me?" gasped Beth.

"Yes, for you," cried Jo, hugging her sister and offering the note. "Don't you think he's the dearest old man in the world?"

"You read it, Jo. I can't, I feel so odd!" And Beth hid her face in Jo's apron, quite upset by her present.

Jo opened the paper and began to laugh, for the first words she saw were:

"'MISS MARCH,

"'Dear Madam,

"'I have had many pairs of slippers in my life, but I never had any that suited me so well as yours. I like to pay my debts, so I know you will allow 'the old gentleman' to send you something which once belonged to the little granddaughter he lost. With hearty thanks and best wishes, I remain,

"'Your grateful friend and humble servant,

JAMES LAURENCE.'"

Beth was trembling. She put out a hand to the piano and touched the beautiful black and white keys, and pressed the shiny pedals.

"You'll have to go and thank him," said Jo, as a joke – for the idea of the child's going never entered her head.

"Yes, I mean to," said Beth. "I'll go now, before I get frightened thinking about it."

To the utter amazement of her family, she walked down the garden, through the hedge and in at the Laurences' door. She went into the house and knocked at the study door before she gave herself time to think.

"Come in!" a gruff voice called.

In she went, right up to Mr Laurence, who looked taken aback, and held out her hand, saying, with only a small quaver in her voice, "I came to thank you, sir, for—"

She didn't finish. He looked so friendly that she forgot her speech and, instead, put both arms round his neck and kissed him.

The old gentleman couldn't have been more astonished if the roof of the house had suddenly flown off. But he liked it. He sat the child on his knee, feeling as if he'd got his own little granddaughter back again, and Beth talked to him as cosily as if she'd known him all her life.

When she went home he walked with her to her own gate, shook hands and touched his hat.

The girls, who'd seen it all, nearly fell out of the window in their surprise. Jo danced a jig to express her satisfaction, while Meg exclaimed, with uplifted hands: "Well, I do believe the world is coming to an end!"

## CHAPTER SIX
# Thin Ice

"Girls, where are you going?" It was Amy who spoke. She'd come into their room one Saturday afternoon and found Meg and Jo getting ready to go out. There was an air of secrecy about them which excited her curiosity.

"Never you mind. Little girls shouldn't ask questions," returned Jo sharply.

Amy bridled at this insult. She turned to Meg, who never refused her anything for long. "Do tell me," she said coaxingly. "I should think you might let me go too."

"I can't, dear, because you aren't invited," began Meg; but Jo broke in impatiently: "Now, Meg, be quiet, or you'll spoil it all. You can't go, Amy, so don't be a baby."

"You're going somewhere with Laurie, I know you are. You were whispering and laughing together on the sofa last night, and you stopped when I came in. Aren't you going with him?"

"Yes, we are. Now do be still and stop bothering!"

Amy held her tongue, but used her eyes and saw Meg slip a fan into her pocket.

"I know! You're going to the theatre," she cried. "And I *shall* go, for I have some money, and it was mean not to tell me in time."

"Just listen to me a minute and be a good child," said Meg soothingly. "Mother doesn't want you to go this week because you've had such a bad cold. Next week you can go with Beth and Hannah, and have a nice time."

"I'd rather go with you and Laurie. Please let me. I've been sick with this cold so long, and I'm dying for some fun. Do, Meg! I'll be ever so good," pleaded Amy.

"Suppose we take her? I don't believe Mother would mind, if we bundle her up well," said Meg.

"If *she* goes, then I shan't," said Jo crossly. "Laurie won't like it; and it will be very rude, after he invited only us, to go and drag in Amy. I should think she'd hate to poke herself in where she isn't wanted."

Her tone and manner angered Amy, who said, in her most aggravating way: "*I shall go*! Meg says I may. If I pay for myself, Laurie hasn't anything to do with it."

"You can't sit with us, for our seats are reserved and you mustn't sit alone. Then Laurie will give you his place and that will spoil things for us. Or he'll get another seat for you, and that isn't proper when you weren't asked. You're not going, so you can just stay where you are," scolded Jo, crosser than ever.

Amy began to cry. Meg had just started to reason with her when Laurie called from below, and the two girls hurried down, leaving their sister wailing. Just as the party were setting out Amy called over the banisters in a threatening tone:

"You'll be sorry for this, Jo March – just wait and see!"

"Fiddlesticks!" returned Jo, and slammed the door.

She enjoyed herself at the theatre, but between the acts she amused herself by wondering what her sister would do to make her "sorry for it". Both she and Amy had quick tempers; and Jo, at least, found it hard to curb the fiery spirit that was continually getting her into trouble.

Amy was reading in the parlour when they got home. She wore an injured look, never lifted her eyes from her

book or asked a single question. On going up to put away her hat, Jo looked towards the bureau; for, in their last quarrel, Amy had turned Jo's drawer upside down on the floor. Everything was still in its place, and Jo decided that Amy had forgiven and forgotten her wrongs.

Next day Meg, Beth and Amy were sitting together in the late afternoon when Jo burst into the room, looking excited, and demanded breathlessly: "Has anyone taken my story?"

Both Meg and Beth looked surprised. "No," they said together.

Amy poked the fire and said nothing. Jo saw her colour rise, and was upon her in a second.

"Amy, you've got it!"

"No, I haven't."

"You know where it is, then!"

"No, I don't."

"That's a fib!" cried Jo, taking her by the shoulders and looking fiercely into her eyes.

"It isn't. I don't know where it is now, and I don't care!"

"You know something about it, and you'd better tell at once or I'll make you," and Jo gave her a slight shake.

Amy was getting excited in her turn. "You'll never get your silly old story again!" she cried.

"Why not?"

"I burnt it up – that's why!"

Jo turned very pale. "What! My little book I was so

fond of and meant to finish before father got home? Have you really burnt it?"

She was horrified. Her hands clutched Amy nervously.

"Yes. I told you I'd make you pay for being so cross yesterday, and so I have, so—"

Amy got no further. Jo's hot temper mastered her and she shook Amy till the teeth chattered in her head, crying, "You wicked girl! I never can write it again, and I'll never forgive you as long as I live!"

Meg flew to rescue Amy, and Beth to pacify Jo; but Jo was quite beside herself, and, with a parting box on her sister's ear, she rushed out of the room and up to the old sofa in the garret, where she finished her fight alone.

The storm cleared up below, for Mrs March came home and, having heard the story, soon brought Amy to a sense of the wrong she had done. Jo's book was the pride of her heart. It was only half a dozen fairy tales, but Jo had worked hard over them, hoping to make something good enough to print. Amy's bonfire had burnt up the work of several years. A small loss to others, to Jo it was a calamity, and she felt that it never could be made up to her.

Jo came downstairs when the tea bell rang.

Amy said meekly: "Please forgive me, Jo. I'm very sorry."

"I never shall forgive you," was Jo's stern answer.

It was not a happy evening. Something was wanting, and the sweet home peace was disturbed.

As Jo received her good-night kiss, Mrs March whis-

pered gently: "My dear, don't let the sun go down upon your anger. Forgive each other, help each other, and begin again tomorrow."

Jo shook her head and said gruffly, because Amy was listening, "It was a horrible thing to do, and she doesn't deserve to be forgiven."

With that, she marched off to bed.

Next morning she still looked like a thundercloud. In the afternoon she decided to go out. "I'll ask Laurie to go skating," she said to herself. "He's always kind and jolly, and he'll make me feel better."

Off she went. Amy heard the clash of skates and looked out of the window with an impatient exclamation:

"There! she promised I should go next time," she said. "But it's no use asking such a cross-patch to take me."

"Don't say that," said Meg. "It's hard for Jo to forgive the loss of her book; but I think she might do it now, and I guess she will if you try her at the right minute. Go after them. Don't say anything in front of Laurie, but just go up to Jo and give her a kiss. I'm sure she'll be friends again with all her heart."

Amy's face lit up. "I'll try," she said, and was off at once in a flurry to get ready.

Jo and Laurie were just disappearing over the hill when she left the house. She ran after them.

It was not far to the river, but both were ready before Amy reached them. Jo saw her coming, and turned her

back. Laurie was skating carefully along the shore and sounding the ice, for a warm spell had gone before the cold snap.

"I'll go on to the first bend and see if it's all right before we begin to race," Amy heard him say as she came up.

He shot away.

Jo heard Amy, panting after her run, stamping her feet and blowing on her fingers as she tried to put her skates on; but Jo never turned and went slowly zigzagging down the river, taking a bitter, unhappy sort of satisfaction in her sister's troubles.

As Laurie turned the bend he shouted back: "Keep near the shore. It isn't safe in the middle."

Jo heard, but Amy was just struggling to her feet and did not catch a word.

"I don't care whether she heard or not," thought Jo. "Let her take care of herself."

Laurie vanished round the bend. Jo was just at the turn and Amy, far behind, was striking out towards the smoother ice in the middle of the river. Then something made Jo turn round. She was just in time to see Amy throw up her hands and go down. There was a crash of rotten ice, a splash of water and a cry that made Jo's heart stand still with fear. She tried to push forward, but her feet had no strength. Then something rushed swiftly by her and Laurie's voice cried out:

"Quick! Bring one of those fence rails!"

How she did it, she never knew. For the next few minutes she worked as if possessed, blindly obeying Laurie, who was quite calm and who, lying flat, held Amy up by his arm till Jo dragged a rail from the fence and together they got the child out, more frightened than hurt.

"Now, we must walk her home as fast as we can. Pile our things on her while I get off these confounded skates," cried Laurie, wrapping his coat round Amy and tugging away at the straps of her skates.

Shivering, dripping and crying, Amy was got home. There she fell asleep, rolled in blankets before a hot fire. During the bustle Jo flew about, looking pale and wild, her dress torn and her hands cut and bruised.

When Amy was comfortably asleep, Mrs March, who was sitting by the bed, called Jo to her and began to bind up the hurt hands.

Jo looked at the golden head, which might have been swept away from her sight for ever under the treacherous ice. "Are you sure she's safe?" she whispered.

"Quite safe, dear; she's not hurt and won't even take cold, I think. You were so sensible in covering her and getting her home quickly."

"Mother," said Jo, "if she *should* die, it would be my fault!" Her voice broke. She dropped down beside the bed in tears, telling all that had happened, sobbing out her gratitude for being spared the heavy punishment that might have come upon her.

"It's my dreadful temper!" she sobbed. "I try to cure it. I think I have, and then it breaks out worse than ever. Oh, Mother, what shall I do? Oh, do help me!"

Mrs March drew the tousled head to her shoulder. "I will," she said. "Don't cry so bitterly. Remember this day and make up your mind that you'll never know another like it. You think your temper is the worst in the world, but mine used to be just like it."

Through her tears, Jo stared at her mother in surprise. "Yours, Mother? Why, you are never angry!"

"I've been trying to cure my temper for forty years, and I've only succeeded in controlling it. I'm angry nearly every day of my life, Jo, but I've learned not to show it, and I still hope to learn not to feel it, though it may take me another forty years to do so."

Jo found great comfort in these words. In the silence that followed, Amy stirred in her sleep. Jo looked up with an expression on her face that it had never worn before.

"I was so angry," she said, "that I wouldn't forgive her. Today, if it hadn't been for Laurie, it might have been too late! How could I be so wicked?"

She leaned over her sister, softly stroking the fair hair.

As if she heard, Amy opened her eyes and held out her arms with a smile that went straight to Jo's heart. Neither said a word, but they hugged one another close, in spite of the blankets, and everything was forgiven and forgotten in one hearty kiss.

## Chapter Seven
# *Fine Feathers*

"I do think it's a lucky thing that those children should have the measles just now," said Meg, "because it means that there's no difficulty about my holiday."

It was a day in April, and she stood packing her trunk with the help of her sisters.

"It's very nice of Annie Moffat not to forget her promise. You'll have a whole fortnight of fun," replied Jo, looking like a windmill as she folded skirts with her long arms.

"And such lovely weather!" added Beth, tidily sorting neck and hair ribbons lent for the great occasion.

Meg was to depart on the next day to stay a fortnight with her friend, Annie Moffat.

The Moffats were very fashionable, and simple Meg was rather daunted at first by the splendour of the house and the fine manners of its occupants. However, they were kindly people who soon put their guest at her ease.

It certainly was agreeable, Meg felt, to eat the best of food, drive in a fine carriage, wear her best frock every day, and do nothing but enjoy herself. It suited her very well. She soon began to imitate the manners of those about her, to put on little airs and graces, crimp her hair,

and talk about the fashions as well as she could. The more she saw of Annie Moffat's pretty things, the more she envied her and sighed to be rich. Home, when she looked back on it, seemed very bare and dismal.

Mr Moffat, a fat and jolly gentleman who knew Meg's father, and Mrs Moffat, a fat, jolly lady, made a great fuss of Meg, so that she was in a fair way to having her head turned.

One evening, when the three girls were getting ready for a party, Meg's heart sank as she compared the shabby gown that she had to wear with the fine dresses of the others. Her cheeks burned when she saw the other girls glance at her gown, and then at one another. No one said a word, however; Sallie offered to do her hair and Annie to tie her sash. In these acts of kindness Meg saw only pity for her poverty, and her heart felt very heavy. The hard, bitter feeling was getting pretty bad, when the maid brought in a note and a box of lovely roses, heath and ferns, both addressed to Meg.

"What fun! Who are they from? Didn't know you had an admirer," cried the girls, fluttering about Meg in a high state of surprise.

"The note's from Mother and the flowers from Laurie," said Meg, very grateful that she had not been forgotten.

"Oh, indeed!" said Annie with a funny look, as Meg slipped the note into her pocket.

The flowers had made Meg feel happy again. She laid

by a few ferns and roses for herself, and quickly made up the rest in little bouquets for her friends. When all the rest went to show themselves to Mrs Moffat, she saw a happy, bright-eyed face in the mirror, as she laid her ferns against her rippling hair and fastened the roses in the dress that didn't strike her as being so *very* shabby now.

She enjoyed herself that evening, until, as she was sitting just inside the conservatory, waiting for her partner to bring her an ice, she heard a voice on the other side of the flowery wall: "How old is he?"

"Oh, sixteen or seventeen, I should say," replied another voice.

"It would be a grand thing for one of those girls, wouldn't it?" said the first voice. "Sallie says they're very friendly now and the old man thinks the world of them."

"Mrs M. has her plans, I dare say, early as it is. The girl evidently doesn't think of it yet." The voice was Mrs Moffat's.

"She coloured up quite prettily when the flowers came," said the other voice. "Poor thing, she'd be so nice if she was only got up in style. Do you think she'd be offended if we offered to lend her a dress for Thursday?"

"She's very proud but I don't think she'd mind, for that dowdy dress is all she's got. She may tear it tonight, and that will be a good excuse for offering a decent one."

"We'll see. I shall ask that Laurence to come, and we'll have fun about it afterwards."

Here Meg's partner returned to find her looking flushed and angry. She tried to forget the gossip she had heard, but could not. Those foolish words had suggested that her mother was planning to see Meg married to Laurie, who would be rich when his grandfather died.

Next morning something in the manner of her friends struck Meg at once. They treated her with more respect, she thought, and looked at her with eyes that betrayed curiosity. All this surprised and flattered her, though she did not understand it till one of Annie's older sisters, Belle, looked up from her writing table and said: "Meg, dear, I've sent an invitation to your friend Mr Laurence for Thursday. We should like to know him."

Meg coloured, but answered mischievously: "You're very kind, but I'm afraid he won't come."

"Why not?" asked Miss Belle.

"He's too old."

"What do you mean? What *is* his age?"

"Nearly seventy, I believe," answered Meg, looking down to hide the merriment in her eyes.

"You sly creature! We meant the young man, of course!" exclaimed Miss Belle, laughing.

"There isn't one. Laurie is only a little boy," answered Meg, then laughed at the look that the sisters exchanged.

"He's about your age," said Annie.

"Nearer my sister Jo's. *I* am seventeen in August," returned Meg, tossing her head.

"It's very nice of him to send you flowers, isn't it?" asked Annie, looking wise.

"Yes, but he often does, to all of us. My mother and old Mr Laurence are friends, you know, so it's quite natural that we children should play together."

Nothing more was said, for Mrs Moffat lumbered in, like an elephant, in silk and lace. "I'm off shopping," she said. "Can I get anything for you, young ladies?"

"Not for me," replied Sallie. "I've got my new pink silk for Thursday, and don't want a thing."

"Nor I—" began Meg, but stopped, thinking that she *did* want several things and could not have them.

"What shall you wear?" asked Sallie.

"My evening dress again, if I can mend it fit to be seen. It got torn last night," said Meg, trying to speak easily.

"Why don't you send home for another?" said Sallie, who couldn't see much beyond the end of her nose.

"I haven't got another."

Sallie said in surprise: "Only that? How funny—"

She did not finish, for Belle broke in, saying kindly: "Not at all. There's no need to send home, Meg, even if you have a dozen. I've got a sweet blue silk which I've out-grown, and you'll wear it to please me, won't you, dear?"

"Well, thank you," said Meg, "but I don't mind my old dress, if you don't."

"Let me please myself by dressing you up in style. You'd be a little beauty with just a touch here and there. I shan't

et anyone see you till you are done, and then we'll burst
upon them like Cinderella and her godmother," said Belle
in her most persuasive tone.

Meg could not refuse. She now very much wanted to
see if she would be "a little beauty" after touching up.

On the Thursday evening Belle shut herself up with
her maid, and between them they turned Meg into a
fine lady. They crimped and curled her hair, they pol-
ished her neck and arms with some fragrant powder, and
touched up her lips to make them redder. They laced
her into a sky-blue dress – so tight that she could hardly
breathe – added bracelets, necklace, brooch and even
earrings. A pair of high-heeled blue silk boots satisfied
the last wish of Meg's heart. A lacy handkerchief, a
plumed fan and a bouquet in a silver holder finished her
off. Miss Belle looked at her with the satisfaction of a
little girl with a newly dressed doll.

"Come and show yourself," she said, and led the way
downstairs.

They sailed into the drawing room. Meg created a mi-
nor sensation. Several young ladies who had taken no
notice of her before now flocked to her; several young
gentlemen who had only stared at her at previous parties now hurried to be introduced.

Meg was flirting her fan and laughing at the feeble jokes
of the young gentlemen when she suddenly stopped
laughing and looked confused. Laurie was sitting just

opposite, staring in surprise. He bowed and smiled, but something in his honest eyes made her blush and suddenly wish she had her old dress on.

Then she rustled across the room to shake hands with him. "I'm glad you came," she said, with her most grown-up air.

"Jo wanted me to come and tell her how you looked," he answered, without turning his eyes upon her.

"What will you tell her?" asked Meg.

"I shall say I didn't know you. You look so grown-up and unlike yourself that I'm quite afraid of you," he said.

"How absurd!" said Meg. "The girls dressed me up for fun, and I rather like it. Wouldn't Jo stare if she saw me?"

She wanted to make him say he thought she looked beautiful.

"Yes, I think she would," returned Laurie gravely.

"Don't you like me so?" asked Meg.

"No, I don't," was the blunt reply.

"Why not?" – in an anxious tone.

He looked her up and down. "I don't like fuss and feathers," he said.

Meg flushed. "You are the rudest boy I ever met!" she said angrily, then turned and walked away.

She went and stood at a quiet window to cool her cheeks, for the tight dress gave her a brilliant colour. As she stood there, a middle-aged man whom she knew passed by and she heard him say to his wife:

"They're making a fool of that little March girl. They've spoilt her. She's nothing but a doll tonight."

Meg felt drowned in shame. She leaned her forehead on the cool pane, until someone touched her arm. She turned. It was Laurie, who said, with his best bow and his hand out:

"I'm sorry for my rudeness. Come and dance with me."

Meg tried to look offended, but failed. She smiled and relented, and, as they stood waiting to catch the time, she whispered: "Take care my skirt doesn't trip you up. It's the plague of my life, and I was a goose to wear it."

"Pin it round your neck, and then it will be useful," said Laurie, looking down at the little blue boots, which he seemed to like.

Away they went, fleetly and gracefully, feeling more friendly than ever after their tiff.

"Laurie, please don't tell them at home about my dress tonight," said Meg, as they danced. "It will worry Mother. I'll tell them all about it myself and how silly I've been. You won't tell, will you?"

"I give you my word I won't – only, what shall I say when they ask me?"

"Just say I looked nice and was having a good time."

"You don't look as if you're having a good time," said Laurie. "Are you?"

"No, not now. I only wanted a little fun, but I'm tired of it now."

The dance ended, and Meg was carried off by another young man. Laurie did not speak to her again till supper, when he saw her drinking champagne with two young men.

"You'll have a splitting headache tomorrow if you drink much of that, Meg" he whispered to her.

"I'm not Meg tonight," she answered. "I'm a 'doll' who does all sorts of crazy things. Tomorrow I shall put away my 'fuss and feathers' and be good again."

For the rest of the evening she danced and flirted, chattered and giggled, and romped through the dances. She kept far away from Laurie till he came to say good night.

"Remember your promise," she said, trying to smile, for the splitting headache had already begun.

"I shall be as silent as the grave!" said Laurie theatrically, and went away.

Meg was sick all the next day, and on Saturday went home, feeling quite used up with her fortnight's fun.

"Home *is* a nice place," she said, as she sat with her mother and Jo on the Sunday evening.

"I was afraid it would seem dull and poor to you after your fine time," replied her mother.

Meg had told them what a charming time she had had, but her mother was quick to notice that something still seemed to weigh on her spirits. When the clock struck nine and Jo rose for bed, Meg left her chair and, taking Beth's stool, leaned her elbows on her mother's knee.

"Mother," she said, "I want to tell you something."

"I thought so. What is it, dear?"

"Shall I go away?" asked Jo.

"Of course not. Don't I always tell you everything? I want you to know all the dreadful things that I did at the Moffats'."

"We're ready," said Mrs March, smiling but looking a little anxious.

"I told you they dressed me up – but I didn't tell you that they powdered and squeezed and frizzled, and made me look like a fashion plate. They said I was a beauty, so I let them make a fool of me."

"Is that all?" asked Jo.

"No. I drank champagne, and romped, and tried to flirt, and was altogether horrid," said Meg.

Mrs March looked at her. "There's something more, I think," she said.

"Yes, there is," Meg answered. "It's very silly, but I want to tell it because I hate to have people think such things about us and Laurie."

She went on to tell about the bits of gossip she had heard at the Moffats'.

"Forget that foolishness," said Mrs March gravely, when her daughter had finished. "I am more sorry than I can say for the mischief this visit may have done, Meg."

"Don't be sorry. I won't let it hurt me. But, tell me, Mother, do you have 'plans' for us, as Mrs Moffat said?"

"Yes, my dear, I have a great many. All mothers do. I want my daughters to be beautiful and good; to be well and wisely married, and to lead useful, pleasant lives. I don't want you to marry rich men simply because they are rich and have fine houses. I'd rather see you poor men's wives as long as you were happy and content."

"Belle says that poor girls don't stand any chance unless they put themselves forward," sighed Meg.

"Then we'll just have to be old maids," said Jo stoutly.

"Right, Jo. Better be happy old maids than unhappy wives," said Mrs March decidedly. "And do remember that I'm always ready to hear your troubles and help you if I can. Remember that Father is always ready to be your friend; and the two of us trust and hope that our daughters, whether married or single, will be the pride and comfort of our lives."

"We will, Mother, we will!" cried both girls with all their hearts, as she fondly wished them good night.

## CHAPTER EIGHT
### *Secrets*

October had come round once more. The days were growing chilly, and the afternoons were short.

Jo was busy up in the garret, seated on the sofa, writing

away with her papers spread out on a trunk before her. When the last page was filled, she signed her name with a flourish and exclaimed: "There! I've done my best! If this doesn't suit I shall have to wait till I can do better."

She lay back on the sofa, read the manuscript carefully through, then tied it up with a smart red ribbon and sat a minute looking at it with a wistful expression. Her desk was an old tin box in which she kept her papers and a few books. She took another manuscript from this box and, putting both in her pocket, crept quietly downstairs.

She put on her hat and jacket as noiselessly as possible, went to the back-entry window, got out on the roof of a low porch, swung herself down to a grassy bank and took a roundabout way to the road that led into town.

Once she was in town, she walked at a great pace till she reached a certain number in a certain busy street. Having found the place she wanted, she went into the doorway, looked up the dirty stairs and, after standing stock-still a minute, suddenly dived into the street and walked away again as rapidly as she had come.

She did this several times, to the great amusement of Laurie, who was leaning in the window of a building opposite. On returning for the third time, Jo gave herself a shake and walked up the stairs, looking as if she was going to have all her teeth out.

There was a dentist's sign at the entrance. Laurie stared at this for a moment, then put on his coat, took his hat

and went down to post himself in the opposite doorway.

"It's like her to come alone," he said to himself, "but if she had a bad time she'll need someone to help her home."

It was ten minutes before Jo came running downstairs. Her face was red and she had the look of a person who has just had a trying time. When she saw Laurie, she did not look pleased and passed him by with a nod. He went after her, asking, with an air of sympathy:

"Did you have a bad time? Was it painful?"

"Not very."

"You got through quickly."

"Yes, thank goodness!"

"Why did you go alone?"

"Didn't want anyone to know."

"You're the oddest fellow I ever saw. How many did you have out?"

Jo looked at her friend as if she did not understand him, then began to laugh as if greatly amused at something. "There are two that I've got to have out, but not until next week."

"What are you laughing at?" said Laurie, looking mystified. "You're up to some mischief, Jo."

"So are you. What were you doing in that billiard room?"

"Begging your pardon, ma'am, it isn't a billiard room. It's a gymnasium, where I take lessons in fencing."

"Well, I'm glad about that," said Jo. "I don't want to have to start worrying about you."

"Do you worry about me, Jo?"

"A little, when you look moody, as you sometimes do. You've got such a strong will. If you once get started wrong, I'm afraid it would be hard to stop you."

Laurie walked on in silence. Jo watched him, wishing she had held her tongue, for his eyes looked angry, though his lips still smiled as if at her warning.

"Are you going to lecture me all the way home?" he asked at last.

"Of course not. Why?"

"If you are, I'll take a bus. If you're not, I've got something very interesting to tell you."

"What is it?" asked Jo.

"It's a secret – and if I tell you, you must tell me yours."

"I haven't got any—" Jo began, but stopped suddenly, remembering that she had.

"You know you have. You can't hide anything, so own up, or I won't tell," cried Laurie.

"Is your secret a nice one?"

"It is! And all about people you know. I've been wanting to tell you for a long time. Come on, you begin."

"You won't tell at home, will you?"

"Not a word."

"And you won't tease me?"

"I never tease."

"Oh yes, you do. You get all you want out of people. I don't know how you do it, but you're a born wheedler."

"Thank you. Fire away!"

"Well, I've left two stories with a newspaper man, and he's going to give his answer next week," whispered Jo.

"Hurray for Miss March, the celebrated author!" cried Laurie, throwing up his hat and catching it again.

"Be quiet! I don't expect it will come to anything, but I couldn't rest till I'd tried. I said nothing about it because I didn't want anyone else to be disappointed."

"Your stories are much better than half the rubbish that's published every day," said Laurie warmly. "Won't it be fun to see them in print, and shan't we feel proud of our American author?"

Jo's eyes sparkled. It's always pleasant to be believed in, and a friend's praise is always sweet. "What's *your* secret?" she asked. "Play fair, or I'll never believe you again."

Laurie's eyes twinkled. "I know where Meg's glove is – the one she lost at our house last month."

Jo looked disappointed. "Is that all?" she said.

"Yes, but I haven't told you where it is."

"Tell me, then."

"It's in Brooke's pocket."

Jo stopped and stared at him for a minute, looking both surprised and displeased, then walked on, saying sharply: "How do you know?"

"I saw it. Isn't it romantic?"

"No," said Jo, "it's horrid."

"Don't you like it?"

"No, of course I don't. It's ridiculous. Why doesn't he give the glove back? I wish you hadn't told me."

"I thought you'd be pleased."

"At the idea of anybody coming to take Meg away? No, thank you."

"You'll feel better about it when somebody comes to take you away."

"I'd like to see anyone try it," cried Jo fiercely.

"So should I," said Laurie, and chuckled at the idea. "Let's race down this hill – then you'll feel a lot better."

There was no one in sight. Jo darted away, soon leaving hat and hairpins behind her. Laurie was first at the bottom of the hill and turned as Jo came panting up with flying hair, bright eyes and ruddy cheeks.

"I enjoyed that," she said, "but look what a mess I'm in. Go and pick up my things, there's a good boy!"

She dropped down under a maple tree that was carpeting the bank with crimson leaves.

Laurie went off to recover the lost property, and Jo bundled up her hair, hoping no one would pass till she was tidy again. But someone did come along – Meg.

"What are you doing here?" Meg asked in surprise.

"Getting leaves," answered Jo in a meek voice.

"And hairpins," added Laurie, throwing half a dozen into Jo's lap. "They grow on this road, Meg. So do brown straw hats."

"You've been running, Jo. How could you? When *will* you stop your romping ways?" said Meg.

"Never till I'm stiff and old, and have to use a crutch," said Jo. "I don't want to grow up before my time."

Her face looked troubled. Laurie saw it and drew Meg's attention from it by asking quickly:

"Where have you been calling, all so fine?"

"At the Gardiners', and Sallie has been telling me all about Belle Moffat's wedding. It was very splendid, and they've gone to spend the winter in Paris. How wonderful that must be!"

"Do you envy her, Meg?" said Laurie.

"I'm afraid I do."

"I'm glad of it," muttered Jo.

Meg looked surprised. "Why?" she asked.

"Because if you care so much about riches, you'll never go and marry a poor man," said Jo, frowning at Laurie, who was trying to warn her to mind what she said.

"I shall never *go* and marry anyone," said Meg, and walked on with great dignity.

For a week or two Jo behaved so oddly that her sisters got quite bewildered. She rushed to the door when the postman rang; she was rude to Mr Brooke whenever they met; she would sit looking at Meg with a sad face; and she and Laurie were always making signs to one another, till the girls declared that they had both lost their wits.

Two Saturdays later, Meg, as she sat sewing at the win-

dow, was scandalised by the sight of Laurie chasing Jo all over the garden. He finally captured her behind a laurel bush. What went on there Meg could not see, but shrieks of laughter were heard, followed by the murmur of voices and a great flapping of newspapers.

"When will that girl behave like a young lady?" sighed Meg to herself.

In a few minutes Jo bounced in, laid herself on the sofa and pretended to read.

"Have you anything interesting there?" asked Meg.

"Only a story. It's not much good, I guess," returned Jo, carefully keeping the name of the paper out of sight.

"You'd better read it aloud," said Amy. "It will amuse us and keep you out of mischief."

"What's it called?" asked Beth, wondering why Jo kept her face behind the sheet.

"The Rival Painters."

"It sounds good," said Meg. "Read it, Jo."

"Hem!" said Jo and took a long breath. She began to read. The girls listened with interest, for there was something in Jo's voice that caught their attention.

Jo came to the end at last. She lowered the paper. Beth looked at her face.

"Who wrote it?" she asked.

The reader suddenly sat up, threw away the paper and replied in a loud voice, "Your sister."

"You?" cried Meg, dropping her work.

"It's *very* good," said Amy.

"I knew it! I knew it!" cried Beth. "Oh, Jo, I *am* so proud!" and she ran to hug her sister.

How delighted they all were, to be sure. How they stared at the words "Miss Josephine March" actually printed in the paper. How Hannah came in to exclaim, "Sakes alive, well I never!" And how proud Mrs March was.

Jo told them how she had taken her stories to the newspaper office. She added: "And when I went to get my answer, the man said he liked them both but didn't pay beginners, only let them print in his paper. And when the beginners improved, anyone would pay. So I let him have the two stories, and today this was sent to me. And now I shall write more, and get the next one paid for; and oh! – I *am* so happy!"

And wrapping her head in the newspaper, Jo shed a few tears on her little story, which promised to be the first step towards so much that lay in the future.

## CHAPTER NINE
# *A Telegram*

"November is the most disagreeable month of the year," said Meg gloomily. She was standing at the window one dull afternoon, looking out at the frostbitten garden.

"If something very pleasant should happen now we should think it a delightful month," said Beth, who took a hopeful view of everything, even November.

"Nothing pleasant ever *does* happen in this family," said Meg, who was out of sorts.

"Jo and I are going to make fortunes for you all," said Amy. "Just wait ten years, till she's a famous author and I'm a brilliant artist."

"Can't wait till then," said Meg. She sighed and turned once more to the frostbitten garden. Jo groaned and leaned both elbows on the table despondently, and Beth, who sat at the other window, said with a smile: "Two pleasant things are going to happen right away: Mother is coming down the street, and Laurie is tramping through the garden as if he had something nice to tell."

In they both came, Mrs March with her usual question: "Any letter from Father, girls?"

When the girls had shaken their heads, Laurie said:

"Will some of you come for a drive? I've been pegging away at maths till my head's all in a muddle. Come on, Jo, you and Beth will come, won't you?"

"We three will be ready in a minute," cried Amy, running away to wash her hands.

" Can I do anything for you, Mrs March?" asked Laurie.

"No, thank you, Laurie, except perhaps call at the post office. It's our day for a letter from Father, but the postman hasn't been. I can't understand why—"

A sharp ring interrupted her. A few seconds after and Hannah came in, holding a telegram.

"It's one of them horrid telegraph things, mum," she said, holding it as if she was afraid it would explode.

Mrs March snatched it, read it and dropped back into her chair, as white as if it had sent a bullet to her heart. Laurie dashed for water, while Meg and Hannah supported her, and Jo read aloud in a frightened voice:

"MRS MARCH:
"Your husband is very ill. Come at once.
                        "S. HALE,
                            "Service Hospital, Washington."

The day seemed suddenly to have darkened outside. The girls gathered anxiously about their mother.

"I must go to Father at once," she said, "but it may be too late."

The girls began sobbing at these words.

"I won't waste no time a-cryin', but git your things ready right away, mum," said Hannah, and went away to work like three women in one.

"She's right. This is no time for tears," said Mrs March, looking pale but steady. "Let me think. Where's Laurie?"

"Here, ma'am. What can I do?"

"Send a telegram saying that I will come at once. Take a note to Aunt March's. Jo, give me that pen and paper."

Jo did so, knowing that money for the long, sad journey

must be borrowed from Aunt March and feeling as if she would do anything to add a little to the sum.

Mrs March handed the note to Laurie. "Don't kill yourself driving at a desperate pace." she said.

Laurie dashed out and, five minutes later, tore by the window on his own fast horse, riding as if for his life.

While Meg and Amy helped their Mother, Jo was sent to the chemist's to buy a long list of things and Beth was sent round to old Mr Laurence.

"Ask him," said Mrs March, "for a couple of bottles of old wine. I'm not too proud to beg when Father's life is at stake."

Mr Laurence came hurrying back with Beth, offering to help in a dozen different ways. He even offered himself as escort to Washington, but Mrs March would not hear of the old gentleman's undertaking the long journey. He marched away, saying he'd be back directly. Five minutes later Mr Brooke appeared and Meg let him in.

"I'm very sorry to hear of this, Miss March," he said in his pleasant voice. "I've come to offer myself as escort to your mother. Mr Laurence is sending me there on business, and I shall be most pleased to be of service to her."

Meg put out her hand, her eyes shining. "Thank you so much," she said. "Mother will accept, I'm sure."

Something in his brown eyes made her look down hurriedly and lead the way into the parlour, saying she would call her mother.

The short afternoon wore away. Everyone else was busy, but still Jo did not come back. They began to get anxious, and Laurie went off to find her. He missed her, however, and she came walking in with a strange look on her face, which puzzled the family as much as did the roll of dollar bills she laid before her mother.

She said, with a little choke in her voice: "That's to help make Father comfortable and bring him home."

"My dear, where did you get it? Twenty-five dollars! Jo, I hope you haven't done anything rash?"

"No, it's mine honestly. I earned it, and I don't think you'll blame me, for I only sold what was my own."

As she spoke, Jo took off her bonnet. The others cried out. All her abundant hair was cut short.

"Your hair, your beautiful hair! Jo, your one beauty!" they all exclaimed.

Jo shrugged her shoulders and said, rumpling up the brown bush and trying to look as if she liked it, "I was getting too proud of my wig. It will do my brains good to have that mop taken off. I'm satisfied, so please take the money and let's have supper."

"Tell me all about it, Jo," said Mrs March firmly.

"Well, I was wild to do something for Father. Then, in a barber's window, I saw tails of hair with the prices marked. One of them – longer but not so thick as mine – was forty dollars. It came over me that I had one thing to make money out of, and without stopping to think I

walked in, asked if they bought hair and what they would give for mine, and – well, that's about all there is to tell."

"Thank you, my dear," said Mrs March quietly, and something in her face made the girls change the subject.

That night, when Beth and Amy were asleep, Meg lay awake, thinking the most serious thoughts of her young life. Jo lay still, and her sister fancied that she was asleep, till a stifled sob made her exclaim:

"Jo, dear, what is it? Are you crying about Father?"

"No, not now."

"What, then?"

"My air," burst out poor Jo.

It did not sound at all comical to Meg, who put her arms round her sister and held her close.

"I'm not sorry," protested Jo, with a choke. "I'd do it again tomorrow if I could. It's only the vain, selfish part of me that goes and cries in this silly way. Don't tell anyone, Meg. But why are you awake?"

"I can't sleep – I'm so anxious."

"Think about something pleasant."

"I tried it, but felt wider awake than ever."

"What did you think of?"

"Handsome faces – eyes, particularly," answered Meg.

"What colours do you like best?"

"Brown – that is – sometimes – blue are lovely."

Jo laughed, and Meg sharply ordered her not to talk. Soon, they both fell asleep.

The clocks were striking midnight as a figure glided quietly from bed to bed, smoothing a coverlet here, settling a pillow there and pausing to look at each unconscious face. It was Mrs March.

As she lifted the curtain to look out into the dreary night, the moon broke from behind the clouds. It shone upon her like a bright face that seemed to whisper: "Take comfort! There is always light behind the clouds."

## CHAPTER TEN
# *Dark Days*

In the cold grey dawn the sisters lit their lamp. As they dressed they agreed to say goodbye cheerfully and send their mother on her anxious journey unsaddened by tears from them.

Nobody talked much, but, as the time drew near, and they sat waiting for the carriage, Mrs March said to the girls: "Hannah and Mr Laurence will look after you while I'm away, so I have no fears for you. Don't grieve and fret when I'm gone, but go on with your work as usual. Be patient and write to me often—"

The rattle of an approaching carriage made them all start and listen. That was the hard minute, but the girls stood it well. They kissed their mother quietly, clung

about her tenderly, and tried to wave their hands cheerfully when she drove away.

Laurie and his grandfather came over to see her off, as
well as Mr Brooke, who was to travel with her and who
looked, the girls thought, strong and sensible and kind.

"Goodbye, my darlings! God bless you!" whispered Mrs
March, and hurried into the carriage.

"I feel as if there had been an earthquake," said Jo, as
their neighbours went home to breakfast.

"It seems as if half the house was gone," added Meg.

The next hour was a bad one. More than once they
were all on the edge of tears. Hannah, however, bustled
around and came to the rescue armed with a coffee pot.

Three days later there came a letter from their mother.
Father, she said, had been dangerously ill, but was already on the mend. After that a letter came every day,
and the messages grew more and more cheering as the
week passed.

"Meg, I wish you'd go and see the Hummels. You know
Mother told us not to forget them," said Beth, ten days
after Mrs March's departure.

She meant the German family to whom the girls had
given their breakfast on Christmas Day.

"I'm too tired to go this afternoon," replied Meg.

"Can't you, Jo?" asked Beth.

"Too stormy for me, with my cold."

"I thought it was almost better."

"It's not well enough for me to go to the Hummels," said Jo, "and I want to finish this story."

"Why don't you go yourself?" asked Meg.

"I *have* been every day, but the baby is sick and I don't know what to do for it. Mrs Hummel goes out to work, and one of the children takes care of it, but it gets sicker, and I think you or Hannah ought to go. I've got a headache and I'm tired," said Beth, listlessly.

"Amy will be in soon, and she'll run down for us," suggested Meg.

"Well, I'll rest a little and wait for her."

An hour passed and Amy did not come. Meg went to her room to try on a new dress, Jo was lost in her story, and Hannah was sound asleep before the kitchen fire. Beth quietly put on her hood, filled her basket with odds and ends for the poor children and went out into the chilly air with a heavy head and heart.

It was late when she came back, and no one saw her creep upstairs and shut herself in her mother's room. Half an hour later Jo went to "Mother's cupboard" for something and there found Beth sitting by the medicine chest, looking very grave, with red eyes and a camphor bottle in her hand.

"Christopher Columbus! What's the matter with you?" cried Jo.

Beth put out a hand as if to warn her off and asked quickly: "You've had scarlet fever, haven't you?"

"Years ago, when Meg did. Why?"

"Then I'll tell you – oh, Jo, poor Mrs Hummel's baby is dead! It died in my lap," cried Beth, with a sob.

"How dreadful! I ought to have gone," said Jo, sadly.

"It wasn't dreadful, Jo, only so sad! Mrs Hummel had gone for the doctor, so I took the baby on to my lap. It seemed asleep, but all of a sudden it gave a little cry and trembled, and then lay very still. I tried to warm its feet, and give it some milk, but it didn't stir and I–I knew it was dead. I sat and held it till Mrs Hummel came with the doctor. He said it was dead and looked at the other children. Two of them had got sore throats. 'Scarlet fever,' he said crossly; 'ought to have called me before.' Then he turned on me and told me to go home right away or I'd have the fever."

Jo looked frightened at that. She looked at Beth, felt her head, peeped into her throat and then said gravely: "I'm afraid you *are* going to have it, Beth. I'll call Hannah; she knows all about sickness."

Hannah was wide awake in a minute and said that there was no need to worry: everyone had scarlet fever and, if rightly treated, nobody died.

"I'll tell you what we'll do," she said, when she had examined Beth. "We'll have Dr Bangs, just to take a look at you, dear. Then we'll send Amy off to Aunt March's to keep her out of harm's way, and one of you girls can stay at home and look after Beth for a day or two."

"*I* shall, because it's my fault she's sick. I told Mother I'd do the errands, and I haven't," said Jo decidedly.

When Amy was told that she was to go to Aunt March's, she rebelled at once and said that she'd rather have the fever. It was Laurie who persuaded her at last in his most wheedlesome tone, "Now be a sensible girl and do as they say. You go to Aunt March's and I'll take you out every day, driving or walking, or to the theatre. I advise you to be off as soon as you can, for scarlet fever is no joke, miss."

"Will you bring me back the moment Beth is well?"

"The very minute."

"And take me to the theatre, truly?"

"A dozen theatres, if you like."

"Well . . . I guess . . . I will," said Amy slowly.

Beth did have the fever, and was much sicker than anyone but Hannah and the doctor suspected. Meg stayed at home, lest she should infect the children in her charge, and looked after the house. Jo nursed Beth day and night Beth was very patient and bore her pain without complaint, though in a few days when the fever fits began she did not even know the familiar faces around her.

How dark the days seemed now, how sad and lonely the house, and how heavy were the hearts of the sisters as they worked and waited, while the shadow of death hovered over the once happy home. Through it all, Beth lay hour after hour, tossing and turning, with mumbled

words on her lips, or lost in a heavy sleep that brought her no refreshment. Dr Bangs came twice each day. Hannah sat up at night, Meg kept a telegram in her desk all ready to be sent off at any minute, and Jo never stirred from Beth's side.

The first of December was a wintry day indeed to them, for a bitter wind blew and snow fell fast. When Dr Bangs came that morning he looked long at Beth, held the hot hand in both his own a minute, and laid it gently down, saying in a low tone to Hannah: "If Mrs March *can* leave her husband, you'd better send for her."

Hannah nodded without speaking. Meg dropped into a chair, the strength seeming to go out of her legs at the sound of those words, and Jo, after standing with a pale face for a minute, ran to the parlour, snatched up the telegram and, throwing on her things, rushed out into the storm. She was soon back, and while she was taking off her cloak Laurie came in. When he saw Jo's face so full of misery he asked quickly:

"What is it – is Beth worse?"

"I've sent for Mother," answered Jo. "The doctor said we should."

The tears streamed fast down her cheeks. She stretched out a hand in a helpless sort of way, and Laurie took it in his, whispering as well as he could with a lump in his throat: "I'm here, Jo, hold on to me."

She did "hold on", while the boy stood still and silent.

Presently, as Jo's sobs quietened, he said hopefully, "I don't think she'll die. She's so good and we all love her so much, I don't believe God will take her away yet."

Jo stopped crying, for her friend's words cheered her up in spite of her own fears and doubts.

"Cheer up," said Laurie, "and I'll tell you something that will warm the cockles of your heart."

"What is it?" cried Jo.

"I telegraphed to your Mother yesterday, and Brooke answered that she'd come at once. She'll be here tonight. Aren't you glad I did it?"

Jo stared at him until his face reddened. She grew quite white, flew out of her chair, threw her arms round his neck and cried joyfully: "Oh, Laurie, I'm so glad! Tell me why you did it."

"I got fidgety," said Laurie, "and so did Grandpa. We thought your mother ought to know that Beth was ill. She'd never forgive us if – well, if anything happened, you know. So I got Grandpa to say it was high time we did something, and off I pelted to the telegraph office yesterday. Your mother will come, I know – the late train gets in at 2 a.m. tomorrow – and you've only got to keep Beth quiet till she gets here."

"Laurie, you're an angel! How shall I ever thank you?" cried Jo, and then flew from the room to tell Meg and Hannah the good news.

After that a breath of fresh air seemed to blow through

the house. Everything appeared to feel the hopeful change. All day the snow fell, the bitter wind raged and the hours dragged slowly by. Night came at last, and Meg and Jo sat on either side of their sister's bed, thinking that each hour brought help nearer. The doctor had been in to say that some change for the better or worse would probably take place about midnight, at which time he would return.

It was past two when Jo, who stood at the window, heard a movement from the bed. She was by its side in a moment, and, to her excited eyes, a great change seemed to have taken place. The flush and the look of pain were gone, and Beth's face looked pale and peaceful.

Hannah hurried to the bed, looked at Beth, felt her hands, listened at her lips, and then exclaimed: "The fever's turned; she's sleepin' nat'ral. Praise be given! Oh, my goodness me!"

Before the girls could believe the happy truth, the doctor came to confirm it. He smiled at Jo and Meg and said with a fatherly look: "Yes, my dears, I think she'll pull through. For the moment, just let her sleep."

Morning came at last, and never had the world seemed so lovely as it did to the heavy eyes of Meg and Jo as they looked out of the window.

"It's like a fairy world," said Meg, smiling to herself as she stood behind the curtain watching the dazzling sight.

"Hark!" cried Jo, starting to her feet.

Yes, there was a sound of bells at the door below, a cry from Hannah, and then Laurie's voice, saying in a joyful whisper: "Girls, she's come! She's here at last!"

CHAPTER ELEVEN

# Laurie Makes Mischief

There are no words in which to tell of the meeting of the mother and daughters – merely that from that moment on the house was full of happiness.

That same evening, while Meg was writing to Father to report the traveller's safe arrival, Jo slipped upstairs into Beth's room and, finding her mother in her usual place by Beth's side, stood a minute twisting her fingers in her hair with a worried look on her face.

"Well, my dear, what is it?" asked Mrs March quietly.

"Last summer," Jo said, "Meg left a pair of gloves over at the Laurences' – and only one was returned. We forgot all about it, till Laurie told me that Mr Brooke had it. He kept it in his waistcoat pocket and once it fell out. Laurie joked about it, and Mr Brooke owned that he liked Meg but didn't dare say so, since she was so young and he so poor. Now, isn't that a dreadful state of things?"

Mrs March gave her an anxious look. "Do you think Meg cares for him?" she asked.

"Mercy me! I don't know anything about love and such nonsense!" cried Jo. "Meg doesn't *seem* any different."

"Then you think that she's *not* interested in John?"

"Who?" cried Jo, staring.

"Mr Brooke. I call him 'John' now – we fell into the way of doing so at the hospital, and he likes it."

"Oh dear! I know you'll take his part. He's been good to Father, and you'll let him marry Meg if he wants to! Let's send him about his business," said Jo decidedly, "and not tell Meg a word of it."

"Meg is only seventeen," said Mrs March. "If she and John love each other, they can wait and test the strength of their love by doing so. I hope things will go happily with her. Now, do be quiet, for I hear her coming."

Next day Jo's face was a study, for the secret weighed upon her, and she found it hard not to look mysterious and important. Laurie, indeed, was soon able to coax it out of her, and was at once indignant that he'd not been taken into his tutor's confidence. He set his wits to work to devise some proper punishment for the slight.

Meg, meanwhile, had apparently forgotten the matter. Then a change seemed to come over her, and for a day or two she was quite unlike herself. She started when spoken to, and blushed when looked at.

Jo, one day, came in with a note in her hand. "Here's a note for you, Meg, all sealed up," she said. "It was lying inside the front door. The postman must have left it."

Meg took the note, blushed and started reading it.

Mrs March and Jo were deep in their own affairs when a sound from Meg made them look up. She was staring at the note with a frightened face.

"What is it?" cried her mother, running to her, while Jo tried to take the paper which had done the mischief.

"It's all a mistake – he didn't send it – oh, Jo, how could you do it?" and Meg hid her face in her hands, crying as if her heart was quite broken.

"Me! What's she talking about? I've done nothing!" cried Jo, bewildered.

Meg's eyes flashed with anger as she pulled a second note, all crumpled, from her pocket and threw it at Jo, saying reproachfully: "You wrote it, and that bad boy helped you. How could you be so rude and so cruel?"

Jo hardly heard her, for she and her mother were reading the note, which was written in a peculiar hand.

"MY DEAREST MARGARET – I can no longer hide my love, and must know my fate before I return. I dare not tell your parents yet, but I think they would consent if they knew that we adored one another. Mr Laurence will help me to some good place, and then, my sweet girl, you will make me happy. I beg you to say nothing to your family yet, but to send just one word of love by Laurie to your devoted

                                                    "JOHN."

"Oh, the villain!" cried Jo. "I'll go over and see him right away."

She turned to go, but her mother said, "Wait a minute, Jo, you must clear yourself first. Have you had a hand in this?"

"No, Mother, on my word! If I *had* taken a part in it, I'd have done better than this and written a much more sensible note. I should think anyone would know Mr Brooke wouldn't write such stuff as that," she added scornfully.

"It's like his writing," faltered Meg, comparing it with the note in her hand.

"Oh, Meg, you didn't answer the first one?" cried Mrs March quickly.

"Yes, I did!" Meg hid her face, overcome with shame.

"Tell me the whole story," said Mrs March, sitting down by Meg yet keeping hold of Jo lest she would fly off.

"Laurie gave me the first letter, and looked as if he didn't know anything about it," began Meg, without looking up. "I was worried at first and meant to tell you, then I remembered how you liked Mr Brooke, so I thought you wouldn't mind if I kept my little secret for a few days. Forgive me, Mother, I'm paid for my silliness now. I can never look him in the face again."

"What did you say to him?" asked Mrs March.

"I only said I was too young to do anything about it yet and that he must speak to Father. I could be his friend, but nothing more, for a long while to come."

Mrs March smiled, as if well pleased. Jo clapped her

hands and exclaimed, with a laugh: "Go on, Meg. What did he say to that?"

"He wrote back and told me that he'd never sent any love letter at all, and is sorry that my sister Jo should take such liberties with our names. It's a very kind note, but think how dreadful for me."

Meg looked the image of despair, and Jo tramped about the room, calling Laurie names. All of a sudden she stopped, caught up the two notes, and, after looking at them closely, said decidedly: "I don't believe Brooke ever saw either of these letters. Laurie wrote both."

"Will you go and fetch him, Jo?" said Mrs March. "I'll get to the bottom of this and put a stop to such pranks."

Away ran Jo, and Mrs March gently told Meg Mr Brooke's real feelings.

"Now, dear, what are your own?" she asked. "Do you love him enough to wait till he can make a home for you or will you keep yourself quite free for the present?"

"I've been so scared and worried that I don't want to have anything to do with love for a long while," answered Meg. "If John *doesn't* know anything about this nonsense, don't tell him, and make Jo and Laurie hold their tongues. I won't be deceived and made a fool of – it's a shame!"

When Laurie's step was heard in the hall, Meg fled to the study and Mrs March received the culprit alone.

Jo marched up and down the hall like a sentry, having some fear that the prisoner might bolt. The sound of

oices in the parlour rose and fell for half an hour, but
what happened during that interview the girls never knew.
When they were called in, Laurie was standing by their
mother with such a sorry face that Jo forgave him on the
spot but did not think it wise to betray the fact. Meg
received his humble apology and was much comforted
to be told that Brooke knew nothing of the joke.

"I'll never tell him to my dying day," said Laurie ear-
nestly.

## CHAPTER TWELVE
## The Last Drop

Like sunshine after storms were the peaceful weeks that
followed. The invalids improved rapidly and Mr March,
in his letters, began to talk of returning early in the New
Year.

Beth was soon able to lie on the study sofa all day and
amuse herself with sewing. Meg cheerfully blackened and
burnt her white hands cooking for her sick sister, while
Amy, who had come home again, was on her best be-
haviour.

As December wore on, Jo and Laurie made all sorts of
wild plans for celebrating this unusually merry Christmas. Laurie wanted to have bonfires and skyrockets, and

there were always explosions of laughter when he and Jo got together.

Several days of mild weather ushered in a splendid Christmas Day. Mr March wrote that he would soon be with them. Beth felt very well that morning and, wrapped in her mother's gift – a soft, red, woollen dressing gown – was carried in triumph to the window to see the snowman, loaded with presents, which Jo and Laurie had made in the garden.

How Beth laughed when she saw it, how Laurie ran up and down to bring in the gifts, and what ridiculous speeches Jo made as she presented them.

"I'm so full of happiness that if Father only were here I couldn't hold one drop more," said Beth, sighing with contentment as Jo carried her off to the study to rest after the excitement.

"So am I," added Jo.

"I'm sure I am," echoed Amy.

"And of course I am," cried Meg, smoothing the silvery folds of her first silk dress, which Mr Laurence had insisted on giving her.

"How can *I* be otherwise?" said Mrs March gratefully, her eyes going from her husband's letter to Beth's smiling face.

Now and then, in this workaday world, things do happen in storybook fashion, and what a comfort that is. Half an hour after everyone had said they were so happy

they could hold only one drop more, the drop came.

Laurie suddenly opened the parlour door and popped his head in. There was so much excitement on his face, and his voice was so joyful that he might just as well have uttered an Indian war whoop. Everyone jumped up, though he only said in a queer, breathless voice: "Here's another Christmas present for the March family."

Before the words were well out of his mouth he was whisked away somehow, and in his place appeared a tall man, muffled up to the eyes, leaning on the arm of another tall man, who tried to say something and couldn't. Of course there was a general stampede, and for several minutes everybody seemed to lose their wits. Mr March was hidden in the embrace of four loving pairs of arms; Jo nearly fainted away; Mr Brooke kissed Meg entirely by mistake, as he somewhat incoherently explained; and Amy tumbled over a stool and, never stopping to get up, hugged and cried over her father's boots. Mrs March was the first to recover herself and held up her hand with a warning: "Hush! Remember Beth!"

She was too late. The study door flew open and Beth ran straight into her father's arms. Never mind what happened just after that; for all the full hearts overflowed and there were tears of joy on every side . . . .

It was not all romantic – a hearty laugh set everybody right again, for Hannah was found behind the door, sobbing over the fat turkey that she had forgotten to put

down when she rushed in from the kitchen. As the laughter died away, Mrs March began to thank Mr Brooke for his care of her husband; at which Mr Brooke suddenly remembered that Mr March needed rest and, seizing Laurie, hastily left. Then the two invalids were ordered to rest, which they did by both sitting in one big chair and talking hard.

Mr March told how he had longed to surprise them, how, when the fine weather came, he had been allowed by the doctor to take advantage of it, and how kind and devoted Mr Brooke had been. Mr March paused a minute just there and, after a glance at Meg, who was violently poking the fire, looked at his wife with an inquiring lift of the eyebrows. Mrs March gently nodded her head and asked, rather abruptly, if he wouldn't have something to eat.

There never *was* such a Christmas dinner as they had that day. Hannah's fat turkey was a sight to behold – stuffed, browned and decorated. So was the plum pudding, which quite melted in one's mouth.

Mr Laurence and his grandson dined with them; also Mr Brooke, at whom Jo glowered darkly, to Laurie's great amusement. They drank healths, told stories, sang songs and had a thoroughly good time. A sleigh ride had been planned, but the girls would not leave their father, so the guests departed early, and, as twilight gathered, the happy family sat together round the fire.

"Just a year ago we were groaning over the dismal Christmas we expected to have. Do you remember?" asked Jo.

"I think it's been a pretty hard year," said Amy, with thoughtful eyes.

"It seems to have worked its changes," said Mr March, looking with fatherly satisfaction at the four young faces round him. "I've made several discoveries today."

"Tell us what they are!" cried Meg, who sat beside him.

"Here is one!" he said, taking up the hand that lay on the arm of his chair. He pointed to the roughened forefinger, a burn on the back and two or three little hard spots on the palm. "I remember a time when this hand was white and smooth, and your first care was to keep it so. It was pretty then, but to me it is much prettier now, for in these marks I read a little history. They tell me that Meg has thrown aside her vanity, and I'm sure the sewing done by these pricked fingers will last a long time, so much goodwill went into the stitches. Meg, my dear, I'm proud to shake this good industrious little hand, and hope I shall not soon be asked to give it away."

He squeezed the hand and gave her an approving smile.

"Please say something nice about Jo, for she has tried so hard and been so good to me," said Beth, in his ear.

He laughed and looked across at the tall girl who sat opposite. "In spite of the curly crop, I don't see the 'son Jo' whom I left a year ago," he said. "I see a young lady who pins her collar straight, laces her boots neatly and neither whistles, talks slang nor lies on the rug as she used to do. Her face is thin and pale just now with watching and anxiety, but I like to look at it, for it has grown gentler. I rather miss my wild girl, but if I get a strong, helpful, tenderhearted woman in her place, I shall feel quite satisfied. I don't know whether the shearing sobered our black sheep, but I do know that in all Washington I couldn't find anything beautiful enough to be bought with the five-and-twenty dollars which my good girl sent me."

Jo's thin face grew rosy in the firelight as she received her father's praise.

"Now, Beth," said Amy, longing for her turn but ready to wait.

"There's so little of her I'm afraid to say much, for fear she will slip away altogether, though she is not so shy as she used to be," began their father cheerfully, but remembering how nearly he *had* lost her, he held her close, saying tenderly, with her cheek against his own: "I've got you safe, my Beth, and I'll keep you so, please God."

After a minute's silence he looked down at Amy, who sat at his feet, and said: "I noticed that Amy ran errands for her mother all afternoon, gave Meg her place tonight and has waited on everyone with patience and good humour. I also see that she does not fret much nor strut in front of the mirror. I think she has learned to think of

other people more and of herself less. I'm glad of this and proud of a lovable daughter with a talent for making life beautiful to herself and others."

Their father's kind words had made all the girls feel glad and proud and happy, but the happiest moment for all of them was when Beth slipped out of her father's arms, went to her little piano, softly touched the keys and sang to them in the sweet voice they had never thought to hear again.

## CHAPTER THIRTEEN
# Aunt March Settles the Question

Mr March, next day, was in a fair way to being killed by kindness. His daughters were always at his side. He sat propped up in the big chair by Beth's sofa, with the other three close by, and Hannah popping in her head now and then to "peek at the dear man". Nothing seemed needed to complete their happiness. But something *was* needed, and the elder ones felt it, though none confessed the fact.

Mr and Mrs March looked at one another with anxious expressions as their eyes followed Meg. Jo had sudden fits of gravity and was seen to shake her fist at Mr Brooke's umbrella, which he had left in the hall. Meg was absent-minded, shy and silent, started when the bell rang and coloured when John's name was mentioned.

Laurie went by in the afternoon and, seeing Meg at the window, seemed suddenly to have a fit. He fell down on one knee in the snow, beat his breast, tore his hair and clasped his hands as if begging for some favour. When Meg told him to behave himself and go away, he wrung imaginary tears out of his handkerchief and staggered away as if in utter despair.

"What does the goose mean?" said Meg, laughing and blushing at the same time.

"He's showing you how your John will go on by and by. Touching, isn't it?" answered Jo scornfully.

"Don't say *my* John," said Meg. "It isn't proper or true. I've told you I don't care *much* about him, and there isn't to be anything said, but we are all to be friendly and go on as before."

"We can't," answered Jo, "for *something* has been said. I wish it was all settled. I hate to wait, so if you mean ever to do it, make haste and have it over quick."

Meg bent over her work with a little smile. "I can't say anything till he speaks," she said.

"If he did speak, you wouldn't know what to say. You'd cry or blush or let him have his own way instead of giving a good decided No."

"I'm not so silly or weak as you think. I should merely say, quite calmly and decidedly, 'Thank you, Mr Brooke,

you are very kind, but I agree with Father that I am too young to enter into any engagement at present. So please say no more, but let us be friends as we were.'"

"Hum! That's stiff and cool enough, but I don't think you'll ever say it. You'll give in to him rather than hurt his feelings."

"No, I won't. I shall tell him I've made up my mind, and shall walk out of the room with dignity, like this."

Meg rose as she spoke and moved towards the door, head held high. Then a step and a voice in the hall made her fly to her seat and begin to sew furiously. Jo gave a laugh and turned as there came a knock at the door. It opened and Mr Brooke looked in at them. He seemed a little confused, as his eye went from one face to the other.

"Good afternoon," he said. "I came to get my umbrella – that is, to see how your father is today."

Jo made for the door looking very, very flustered. "It's very well, he's in the rack, I'll get him and tell it you are here," she replied in a hasty manner and slipped out of the room.

The instant she vanished Meg began to sidle toward the door, murmuring: "Mother would like to see you. Please sit down and I'll call her."

Mr Brooke stepped forward, an anxious look on his face. "Are you afraid of me, Margaret? Don't go."

He looked so hurt that Meg thought she must have done something very rude. She blushed and put out her hand,

saying gratefully: "How can I be afraid when you've been so kind to Father? I only wish I could thank you for it."

Mr Brooke held the small hand fast in both his and looked down at Meg with so much love in his brown eyes that her heart began to flutter.

"You can thank me," said Mr Brooke, "if you could give me a little hope, Margaret, if you could say that you care for me a little. I love you so much, my dear."

This was the moment for the calm, proper speech, but Meg didn't make it. She forgot every word of it, hung her head and answered, "I don't know," so softly that John had to stoop down to catch the foolish little reply.

He smiled as if quite satisfied and pressed her hand gratefully. "Will you try and find out?" he said gently.

"I'm too young," faltered Meg, who felt all strange and excited and did not know what to say or do next.

As it happened, however, the door opened and Aunt March came hobbling in at that interesting moment. Meg started as if she had seen a ghost, and Mr Brooke vanished into the study.

"Bless me! What's all this?" cried the old lady.

"It's Father's friend. I'm *so* surprised to see you!" stammered Meg.

"That's clear enough," snapped Aunt March, sitting down. "But what is Father's friend saying to make you blush like a peony? There's mischief going on, and I insist upon knowing what it is!"

"We were merely talking. Mr Brooke came for his umbrella," began Meg.

"Brooke? That boy's tutor? Ah! I understand now. Jo blundered into a wrong message in one of your pa's letters, and I made her tell me. You haven't gone and accepted him, child?" cried Aunt March, scandalised.

"Hush! He'll hear!" said Meg, her face troubled. "Shall I call Mother?"

"Not yet. I've something to say to you. Tell me, do you mean to marry this Cook? If you do, not one penny of my money ever comes to you. Remember that and be a sensible girl."

Meg drew herself up proudly and looked the old lady straight in the eyes. "I shall marry whom I please, Aunt March," she said, "and you may leave your money to anyone you like!"

The old lady glared back at her. "Highty-tighty!" she said. "Is that the way you take my advice, miss? You'll be sorry for it by and by, when you've tried love in a cottage and found it a failure."

"It can't be a worse one than some people find in big houses," retorted Meg.

Aunt March put on her glasses and took a look at the girl, for she did not know her in this new mood. Meg hardly knew herself, she felt so brave and independent, so glad to defend John and assert her right to love him if she liked. Aunt March saw that she had begun wrong, and, after a little pause, said more gently: "Now, Meg, my dear, be reasonable and take my advice. I mean it kindly. You ought to marry well and help your family. It's your *duty* to make a rich match."

"Father and Mother don't think so. They like John, though he *is* poor."

Aunt March took no notice. "So you intend to marry a man without money, position or business? You will have to go on working harder than you do now, when you might be comfortable all your days by minding me and doing better. I thought you had more sense, Meg."

"I couldn't do better if I waited half my life!" Meg exclaimed. "John is good and wise. He's willing to work and sure to get on. Everyone likes and respects him, and I'm proud to think he cares for me, though I'm so poor and young and silly."

"All right!" she cried Aunt March. "I wash my hands of the whole affair! You're a wilful child, and you've lost more than you know by this piece of folly! " She rose and moved towards the door. " No, I won't stay. I wanted to see your father, but I haven't the spirits to talk to him now. I'm disappointed in you! Don't expect anything from me when you're married. I'm done with you for ever."

And slamming the door in Meg's face, Aunt March drove off in high dudgeon. Meg, left alone, stood a moment wondering whether to laugh or cry. Before she could make up her mind, she was taken possession of by Mr

Brooke, who said, all in one breath: "I couldn't help hearing, Meg. Thank you for defending me and thank Aunt March for proving that you *do* care for me a little bit."

"I didn't know how much till she spoke ill of you," said Meg, softly.

"And you'll say yes and make me happy, Margaret?"

"Yes, John," whispered Meg and hid her face on Mr Brooke's waistcoat.

Fifteen minutes later Jo came softly downstairs, paused an instant at the parlour door and, hearing no sound within, nodded and smiled with a satisfied expression, saying to herself: "She has sent him away as we planned. I'll go and hear the fun, and have a good laugh over it."

Poor Jo never got her laugh. She threw open the door and stood transfixed on the threshold, staring with her mouth nearly as wide open as her eyes. The lovers were seated side by side on the sofa. Jo gave a sort of gasp, as if a cold shower had suddenly fallen on her. At the odd sound they turned and saw her. Meg jumped up, looking both proud and shy, but "that man", as Jo called him, actually laughed and said coolly, as he seized the hand of the astonished newcomer: "Sister Jo, congratulate us."

That was adding insult to injury – it was altogether too much. Jo vanished without a word. She went running upstairs, startling the whole household by exclaiming, tragically: "Oh, *do* somebody go down quickly! John Brooke is acting dreadfully, and Meg likes it!"

Mr and Mrs March went down to the parlour at speed, while Jo threw herself on her bed and told the awful news to Beth and Amy. The little girls, however, thought it most interesting, and Jo got little comfort from them, so she went up to the garret to forget her troubles in a book.

A great deal of talking was done in the parlour while Mr Brooke told Meg's parents his plans and persuaded them to arrange everything just as he wanted it.

The tea bell rang before he had finished describing the paradise that he meant to earn for Meg, and he proudly took her in to supper, both looking so happy that Jo hadn't the heart to be jealous or dismal. No one ate much, but everyone looked very happy, and the old room seemed to brighten up amazingly when the first romance of the family began there.

"In most families," said Mrs March, at one point, "there comes, now and then, a year full of events. This has been one for us, but it ends well, after all."

"Hope the next will end better," muttered Jo, who found it hard to see Meg absorbed in a stranger before her face; for Jo loved a few persons very dearly and dreaded to have their affection lost or lessened in any way.

"I hope the third year from this will end better," said Mr Brooke, smiling at Meg, as if everything had become possible to him now.

"Doesn't it seem very long to wait?" asked Amy, who was in a hurry for the wedding.

"I've got so much to learn about keeping a house, it will seem a short time to me," answered Meg gravely.

"You have only to wait. *I* shall do the work," said John, beginning his labours by picking up Meg's napkin, with an expression that caused Jo to shake her head and then say to herself, with an air of relief, as the front door banged: "Here comes Laurie – now we shall have a little sensible conversation."

But Jo was mistaken, for Laurie came prancing into the room in high spirits, holding a bunch of flowers behind his back. He seemed to think that the whole affair had been brought about by his excellent management.

"I knew Brooke would have it all his own way," he said. "He always does. When he makes up his mind to do anything, it's done, though the sky falls." He paused and swept Meg a most theatrical bow, then offered his bouquet with an air. "My congratulations," he said dramatically, "to the future Mrs John Brooke."

Meg took the flowers, all smiles and blushes. Everyone laughed and clapped, and even Jo joined in the merriment, as her eyes went slowly round the room, and brightened as they looked, for the prospect was a pleasant one, and happiness shone from every face.

The year had come to its end; and the ending, after all, had proved a happy one for Mr March's "LITTLE WOMEN".